Cover photo:

Carved figure on the Belvedere, Cimbrone Gardens

Ravello Italy

Staggering On

Christopher Jarman was born in London UK and now lives in Winchester. He spent eight years in the Royal Navy, Fleet Air Arm. He subsequently published many non-fiction educational books during his time as a teacher and lecturer. He has broadcast many talks on the BBC and published over 150 magazine articles on numerous different subjects. He is a qualified pilot and yacht skipper. This book is his seventh novel.

Other novels by Christopher Jarman

Gladd Tidings

Taking Off

Boomcrack

Flotilla

The Libyan Connection

Cocky's Cold War

Grateful thanks to the late Will Rogers for the chapter heading quotes.

First published in Great Britain by Wyke Hill Press Winchester

Second Edition May 2013

STAGGERING ON

Christopher Jarman

Wyke Hill Press

Chapter One

There are two theories to arguing with a woman . . Neither works.

'Don't forget to walk the dog, Peter.'

I heard Sue's voice as in a dream from outside the closing front door. I registered it as someone saying something, but I was concentrating on trying to use nail scissors to cut off a piece of wool that was hanging from my jacket cuff.

Some people say that I have a short attention span; somewhere between a goldfish and a small kitten. That is not entirely true. It's just that I am a teeny weeny bit deaf. Whenever anyone speaks to me, I find it better if they stand directly in front of my head and look me straight in the eyes. People who talk to me from another room, or even more annoying, from outdoors when I am indoors, are wasting their time. Of course, when my brain eventually clicked into today's world, I recalled perfectly what she had said, hence my writing it down accurately.

Sue, my dear wife of sixty years, knows perfectly well that I cannot hear voices from another room or from the back of departing women, but she doesn't hear too well either, and so continues to chat as if we were both 25 years old. Her advantage is that she wants to tell me stuff, but doesn't want to hear anything in return, except presumably, 'Yes dear.'

Mind you, I did hear her clearly last week when she said, from the general area of the washing machine,

'I think you should take at least three pairs of underpants on your next holiday trip.'

I feel sure there was some sort of insult there, but I said nothing.

We watched a television program last week called '56 Up'. It was the eighth program following the progress of a group of seven year old children from different social backgrounds. They made a follow-up program every seven years; you get the idea. I realise now that I missed a golden opportunity to have a film series made of my own life...

Seven Up: Taken to weird Prep School run by defrocked priests and retired cricket players. Close-up of reading to Mr Hudson at his desk while he slid his hand up inside my short trousers and did something strange. I did not mind and thought it was part of learning to read. Mr Hudson was nice and laughed out loud when I told him he looked like a potato. Ran away from this school and my father put me into local Primary school, at that time known as Council Schools, where I was much happier. In those days I could stand on one leg and put on my socks. I could also wear tiny shorts without my tackle appearing below the plimsoll line.

Fourteen Up: Face appears to look like photo of the moon with spots instead of craters. (One day man will walk on the moon says my studious friend Geoffrey, but I do not believe him. Obviously, man would fall off the sides.) Fail to be picked for rugby, cricket or any sport. My biggest ambition is to get extra food at any mealtime. Am curious about girls because am now at an all boys school. Have not spoken to a girl since I was ten. Spend a great deal of time thinking about girl's chests.

Twenty-one Up: My second year as RAF bomber crew. No more spots but pretty decent moustache. I do not actually lie but let most girls assume I am a pilot, but am really the most important member of crew, bomb aimer. After all, how could the pilot bomb Berlin on his own? By now, I have had two girl friends and have done 'it'. But the details need not go into the film, official secrets act and all that. I have also drunk a great deal of beer. If I keep on drinking it, I may get to like it.

Twenty-eight Up: Married to love of life Susan Wilson. I no longer have moustache but very long hair as befits ex-design student now teaching art in suburban secondary modern school. Big row with head of department for teaching 'Modern Art', i.e. getting teenagers to take clothes off and paint not pictures but each others' bodies. Result is promotion to Teacher Training college to continue same methods, thus ruining art education in Surrey for a generation.

Thirty-five Up: Now made Art Inspector for whole county and running highly popular 'body art' courses for art and craft teachers. I write book on 'The New Art' which no-one buys and leave job under a cloud. Live on Sue's wages as English teacher for a year, then obtain work selling encyclopedias door to door. Our first child born, a boy.

You see how the film could go on and be most interesting?

Time to walk Jumble. We call him Jumble because he is exactly as we imagined 'Just William's' dog looked like. We call our cat Korky because of the Dandy comic. You get the picture; we are keen on literary allusions. We named our children the same way. They have come to accept it after all these years, although it was a trifle difficult at first. Our daughter is Scarlett, from the film of course, and our son now quite likes being called Beowulf since he finished paying his debt to society, and to date has a regular job at the re-cycling centre. We called him Bee when he was young, but since he rejoined the actual working population, he has taken to referring to himself as Wulf. He says it fits his character better. But since he is something of a neo-hippie with a tendency to avoid all kinds of confrontation, I think he may be more on the hopeful side there.

Jumble is a difficult dog at the best of times. Sue maintains that he loves his walkies, but I have my doubts. He mopes along the path and sniffs at all the trees and posts etc. almost jerking my arm off. He particularly likes biting (or perhaps sucking would be more accurate, as most of his teeth have dropped out), young children. They always start off by saying 'Nice doggie' and putting their little hands out. Jumble then takes a mouthful of child and tries to hang on. Child then runs to mum shouting with fear. Whacking him with the loose end of his lead does not work as he rather likes this, and apparently considers it the best part of his walk. Jumble prefers to mark his territory on people rather than things like trees or posts. He is particularly attracted to red trouser legs.

On return, I remember that I am supposed to feed Jumble and Korky. Jumble is very excited. I have no idea why a rough little dog would wag its tail almost to extinction at the prospect of some jellied horse. I cut my thumb seriously for the twentieth time when opening the damn tin and have to rush to the kitchen sink and wrap paper towels around the affected digit. I cannot understand why towels these days are always made of paper. In my youth all towels were made of cardboard and much more of a challenge.

Korky, naturally will only eat the gourmet kangaroo and emu sold in little flat plastic packs. These are, if anything, more difficult to open than tins. Using scissors is the only answer, but the clinically approved contents still squirt out of the pack and down my trousers. That's another thing. Why are so many foods and objects 'clinically approved'? What sort of clinic is it that tests horse meat for dogs? Is it the same clinic which tests that toothpaste which is supposed to let you bite ice cubes without flinching?

Jumble has gobbled up the horse chunks including a cupful of my blood with canine relish. Korky has already walked disdainfully out of her cat flap, leaving the food untouched, tail in the air and wiggling her bottom like a pop star on heat. She is ignoring the expensive package meal. I think Alison next door is feeding her. Mind you, I do tend to spoil our little Korky. I have started giving her my portion of Benecol in the mornings. I don't like the taste much myself but hey, it looks like milk and Korky laps it up. If it is clinically proven, to lower my cholesterol, whatever that means, it must completely evacuate the cat of the stuff. Its spiky feline body must be drained of every milligram of cholesterol. I checked on the Internet and Dr Lajos, a cat dietician, said there was nothing bad for a cat in Benecol but she might develop diarrhoea, although a tea spoonful of normal yoghurt would fix it.

Sue returns from her women's club, book study group, or art appreciation whatever. I definitely heard the door open and shut. I can't keep up with the insane drive for knowledge she has developed since turning eighty. It is remarkable for a retired graduate English teacher to believe that she is so poorly educated. When she has learnt all there is to know about Inca art and Worcester porcelain, what does she expect to do with all this information? Perhaps run classes for other old girls in their nineties? She tells me that she is signing up for orientation and map-reading next term.

I put the electric kettle on for a cup of *decaffeinated tea* — yes I know, don't get me started. I remember when electric kettles WERE kettles. My mother had one of the first. That was still a proper kettle. We used to sit round as a family and just gaze at it. It even looked like a kettle. It was made of polished copper and had a decent big black Bakelite plug in the back of it and a lovely curly spout. The one we have now looks as if it might have fallen off the space shuttle. It sits on a circular base ready for take-off. When you fill it up to where it shows three cups, it only pours out two. Maybe it takes a percentage of the water as ullage every time we use it.

We sit at the kitchen table and drink our decaffeinated tea from heavy mugs. Sue may be only a year younger than me but she is still a pretty woman. Her once blonde hair is now white but still looks blond-ish. She wears flowing dreamy sorts of clothes in pastel colours, they make her look like a fairy queen. In fact she is far from languid and can be as rational and as hard as steel when required. We drank from mugs when we were students. Then I started a revolt when we were aged around forty and insisted that we had grown up and should drink out of fine porcelain. This lasted about thirty years, and now we drink tea and coffee out of thick earthquake proof mugs. We don't agree about much but we both like cake. When it comes to religion or books or TV programs, gardening, computers or holidays we find absolutely no common ground. We totally agree about money though. We try not to spend any. On the whole though, we respect each other's eccentricities. As our dear Beowulf always says, 'Even Aesop had his foibles.'

Don't get me wrong, I love Suzy. A sweeter, gentler creature never left a mangled tube of toothpaste on the bathroom windowsill; but she is strange, very strange. Before I was married, I suppose I put women on a sort of pedestal. For example, I thought that all women were naturally more petite and dainty than -well, than men. I thought that they moved as silently as doves around the house and had the appetites of sparrows. That is where bachelors make the mistake of calling girls birds.   They are birds, but quite different varieties from the doves and sparrows.   My wife moves like an eagle around the house, and has the appetite of a vulture just released from a potholing marathon.   I like her to eat mind you, good eaters make good cooks, but it was a surprise, that's all.

Another shock I got was electricity, if you'll excuse the pun. Sue can feel electricity. Yes I know we all get romantic at times and say that sort of thing, after all, courting is still called sparking in Ambridge, so the Archers at least, must have heard about electricity; but my wife can feel much more mundane electricity than that. She says she can tell if the electric iron is connected just by putting her hand on the handle. She can tell if the bedside lamp is plugged in just by touching the lampshade. As a mere male skeptic. I couldn't believe this, but in 50 years she has never been wrong. So now I am convinced. She can feel the stuff.

Then there is this tooth paste thing. It doesn't make sense to me for a grown woman always to press the toothpaste tube at the top every day.   Finally one morning when I was squeezing it myself, I got a palm full of white squidge out of the bottom end. This is not funny.

Another strange thing is the question of tidiness. Here I am extremely fortunate. Many husbands are nagged to a standstill (if my friends are anything to go by) by house-proud wives. In my experience, the normal thing is for men to scatter ash, disarrange cushions and furniture or leave their boots lying about. In our house, it is my wife who leaves her boots and shoes all over the place. She can enter a room and leaves it five minutes later, looking as if someone had tossed a hand grenade in the window and run away. Another thing, I can always tell where she has been sitting, because when she gets up to go there is always a little screwed up ball of handkerchief, either at the back of the seat or on the floor.

You know how small children are rather endearing in the way they will pick up a bright object, look at it, then losing interest open their fingers and let it drop where it lies? Cute, but at 85, Sue is still doing it, with gloves, scarves, hats, occasionally her engagement ring and, ten times a day, her purse. The milkman's eyes have become fixed into round cairngorms of astonishment at the different places from which she eventually produces the milk money; and if anybody says that cairngorms aren't round, then they have not seen our gormless milkman.

I gather too that a lot of wives behave badly in cars. I am not talking about women drivers, that is another subject altogether. Incidentally I did teach my Suzy to drive the car, and with a few finishing lessons from a proper instructor, she passed the test. She was thrilled and delighted. We both were. I hate driving and was overjoyed at the prospect of having a tame if eccentric chauffeuse. That was forty years ago. Since passing the test she hasn't sat in the driver's seat. Apparently, the test was the object and culmination of her desire to drive. She saw no point in it after that. But I was talking about women as passengers. Sue isn't bad, just, well, unusual. She doesn't back seat drive, which is marvellous,. She gets into the car with the kind of expression on her face that I imagine Marie Antoinette must have worn stepping into the tumbrel, or like a sheep going up the ramp at the abattoir. Once inside, she sits with a handkerchief crushed into a ball in her fist. She hangs onto the side of her seat with her he right hand as we start off and waits for me to go round a gentle bend. Whereupon she flings herself to the inside of the bend and grips the door pocket like the passenger in a motorbike and side-car race. This used to terrify me when we were first married. (I didn't notice it when we were engaged) in fact, before we were married Sue wasn't strange at all. She was a perfectly normal very attractive girl. I keep telling her this but she insists that she is just the same and that I am the one who has changed. She says I have become more critical.

Finally, there is this quirk of hers which made me start thinking about these things in the first place. It's drafts. Sorry I should explain, not the black and white checkers kind; I mean the breezes round the houses sort. Sue has this frightful, 'thing' about draughts. It even puts the wind up me at times. If she knows, or even suspects, that there is a door or a window open within fifty yards, she complains of a draft. I then have to traipse off to find it and close it. I suppose it is a kind of blastophobia. Anyway, I can never feel these breezes, but after the electricity business, I took her word for it. Then, the other night, I saw her shivering and looking around again. There was not a door or window in sight that was open and we both knew it. At last, I looked at the television screen and saw that an actor had left a door ajar in the play *and my wife could feel the draught.*

Now I'm convinced she is abnormal. But then, how many wives are normal? And as Sue says quite rightly, "How many husbands are either?"

The next morning I wake up feeling as if a Virgin train has driven back and forth across my body at its usual apathetic pace. My eyelids are glued together like a couple of postage stamps and my neck is calling for help. I have a really heavy weight on my chest which worries me most of all, until I realise that Korky is blissfully napping there. Someone, who shall be nameless, probably me, left the bedroom door open last night.

Walking like a Japanese robot I manage to shuffle towards the shower which is my personal inner sanctum, and I then luxuriate in the hot water which I have set just below the temperature at which flesh roasts. Unfortunately, a person, who shall be nameless, this time not me, runs a bath somewhere down the line, and my carefully calculated shower water turns into hydrochloric acid and rips most of the skin from my back. Not a halcyon start to the day.

Chapter Two

You know you are getting old when everything either dries up or leaks.

Today Sue and I are going to talk, and even communicate if we are lucky, about the BIG PLAN. We are considering emigrating to Italy. No, not just a long holiday, we have already done that; but what our family and friends do not seem to grasp is that we are planning to stay there, buy a house, live there until we die. It is quite simple really, but you would not believe how many people that we know say,

'What, for always?'

'What, in the winter as well?'

'Won't you miss the theatre?'   *Surely you jest!*

'What about the language?'   *non c'è problema!*

'What about Italian cooking?'   *Yum yum*

'Won't you miss English food?' *non c'è problema!*

'Won't you miss the NHS?'

'Hullo! All these are reasons for going in the first place.'

Sue and I have been holidaying abroad ever since the 1960s, France, Spain, America, anywhere we could get a reduced fare or a free trip in return for running courses or summer camps. But mostly we have travelled to Italy and this has become our favourite destination. I have a belief that since the Romans arrived in England nearly two thousand years ago, we are all genetically modified from Italian stock. What else is a British circus ring but a pale descendant of the great Roman Colosseum? Most of our country estates and farms are imitations of Roman detritus. As a child I thought spaghetti only came in tins with tomato sauce. Finally, in Italy, many years later, I discovered that I had been misled. I sympathised with the American tourist in Tuscany whom I once overheard asking, 'Say, do they have pizzas in Italy?'

It wasn't until we had spent some time in Amalfi or on Lake Como that I realised that Italy was the real thing and Britain is a poor imitation, without the wine, the pasta and without the sun. We decided about twenty years ago to spend our last days in Italy. It's just that we haven't got round to it yet. It's now or never.

We each have different ambitions. Sue will soak up the culture, the language, the gardens, and the opera; and I want to lie in the sun and look at the people (well, the girls under 21 mostly.)

We have both been learning Italian, Sue goes to classes and I listen to the Internet. She can hold a conversation on art or music and get any young man to help her with her suitcases. I can order pasta and ask for more Barolo. I know that *basta* means enough, and *prego* means practically anything you want it to. Basically, you can see we are totally in agreement and for all the right reasons. I want her to enjoy culture and stuff. She wants me to be happy and out of her hair.

The problem now is logistics. How do we sell our house and buy another one in a foreign land? Will our pensions be paid over there, and will our savings, such as they are, be available and safe? After all, it's not as if Euros are real money right?

So we sit down to have a conference about it all. This is not the kind of discussion that we used to have many years ago. In those days we could make notes of points in advance, listen to each other's arguments, look one another in the eye and make some rational choices. Nowadays, a meeting consists of me finishing my bowl of muesli while my dear Susie is bustling around doing things with cleaning cloths or dustpans. Most of the time she has her back to me, so I cannot quite hear what she is saying. Sue, bless her, cannot hear me at all. I must remind her to put in her hearing aids. She has them for both ears but insists that she is saving them for later on when   things get really bad. I guess that means when she can no longer hear me shout 'A cuppa would be nice' across the same pillow.

Anyway, we begin by me saying we need to think about selling this *house*. She answers from across the kitchen by saying she has already set a trap for them and why don't I stick to the point?

At this juncture, I give up after only ten seconds of conference time. Then she says,

'Don't forget our daughter Scarlett is a plebeian and we ought not to hold out too much rope.'

Really, I can't imagine what she is actually trying to say. I wish she would learn, after all these years, to speak more clearly. And why say 'our daughter Scarlett'? What am I, eight years old? How many other Scarletts do we know? I agree that we don't see her all that often. She came to visit us for her 50th birthday last year, and brought a very attractive girlfriend with her too. They are running some business together, I don't quite know what; Jenny is her partner. Scarlett is getting too old to settle down and get married. I told her that if she got rid of those dreadful dungarees and put on a dress now and again she could still find a man. But she shot me one of those superior smiles, that adult kids smite you down with, whenever you give them some excellent advice.

That seems to conclude our conference on the Italian job for now. I know we will come back to it again and again because it is like an itch with both of us and also, it seems, to our children. For some reason they have both taken against the idea of Italy. One might have thought that they would be glad to get us out of the way, but it appears that they need our support. Of course to us it is supposed to mean emotional support and strong family ties. I know better. It means to them, financial support and a strong family bank balance.

Only yesterday I had a phone call from my eldest.

'Hi Pop!' he started as usual, 'How's it going?'

Why does everyone begin a phone call in that way? It is so lazy. Surely, a little forethought could produce, 'How's the arthritis?' or 'How's the irritable bowel?' I might then have a chance to talk about something interesting. Anyhow, as it was, I had to say 'Good thanks', which I had learnt from watching Neighbours on the box.

'Look Pop I've got a proposition for you,' said my son. He often has these propositions so I suddenly get canny when I hear those words. It usually means money required. This occasion was no exception.

'What is it going to cost me this week?' I asked.

'No Pop, honestly this is the real thing.'

Well I've heard that before, like a hundred times, but I listened. My little fifty-two year old Beowulf then came up with the idea of the century, according to him,

'I just need a mere five thousand to buy a van and stuff to do *custom carpet cleaning*.'

I was, for the first time in several years, speechless, what the young today call gobsmacked!

'I got an inheritance coming, right?' he said, 'You could take it out of that. Come on Daddy you know it makes sense. Just the one payment and I would be out of your hair for ever.'

If only, I thought. The last time I gave him two thousand out of his dwindling inheritance, it went on paying some woman for a set of healing crystals, which were going to make him a fortune in the ageing hippie medical scene. Well, I was a bit of a hippie myself in the sixties, and I fell for it hook line and whatsit. But of course, the ageing hippie population has evaporated to about seven nowadays; and they have all sold their flower shirts and bell-bottoms and put their trust in the NHS.

I thought deeply about how I could convey my considered views to him tactfully, and then said 'Get stuffed!' and put the phone down. I could not imagine anything else which would be worth saying.

I had to drive down to the yacht club after that, to recover my spirits, and to compare experiences with Dave Bucknell, who had been in the Royal Navy all through the war, so we had something in common. He had three ungrateful kids and virtually no teeth, and understood every nuance of what I said to him.

Over a pint in the bar we compared families for the fiftieth time. He started in his usual way,

'I think it was Dothtoevsky who thaid....'

'Oh for Christ's sake leave your bloody writers out of it,' I shouted. Our conversations often take this turn as Dave had literary pretensions as well as a lisp you could take for a walk.

'I came here to be cheered up and have a drink, not to be lectured on the Russian novel.'

'Well get thith down yer lad – cheerth!' and of course I perked up immediately. No-one could be gloomy with a chum who spoke like that and passed across a large gin and tonic.

'Don't you think that itth great to be alive at thith time of the thentury?'

Dave was far too cheery for my mood and I replied,

'Well, if you think that sitting in the bath each morning trying to cut my toenails and watching an eighty-four year old woman having a pee is great to be alive, then yes, I suppose so.'

Dave is quite a large character with a weathered complexion as befits an ex-navy serviceman. He always wears dark blue trousers and a well-fitting blazer with brass buttons and likes to give the impression that he is still in the 'Andrew' as he refers to his wartime career. In fact, he has spent the last sixty years working for Hampshire County Council as an actuary. I asked him what he did once and he said 'The thame ath an accountant dear boy, but not tho exthiting.'

We both forgot about our families and proceeded to get slaughtered to the extent that I could not possibly drive the 20 miles home and had to stay at the club for the night.

When I got back this morning my dear Sue had not even realised I had gone. She had been watching television until midnight and assumed I had slept in the spare room. It seemed unkind to disabuse her so I said nothing.

It appears that while I was away Sue had been considering how many ways we could find to make some money for the move to Italy.

'We must de-clutter,' she said. 'We have such a lot of stuff that we never use, never look at and don't want. I am sure that if we get someone from Sotheby's down to value it...'

'Just a mo', I said, 'Surely, if we never use the clobber and never look at it and don't want it, what makes you think that anyone else would want to pay good money for the trash, whatever it is?'

'Well, there are those brass pots and trays from Bangalore or Benares or whatever, that your father brought back.'

'Yes, and those prints of old St Albans and the lamps made out of Chianti bottles that your mother gave us,' I countered. 'One all' I then murmured, but she heard me that time and gave me a very wide-eyed look. I added hastily,

'It seems to me that a car boot sale would be more appropriate than a well-known auction house. We could save that for the Renoir and the Picasso in the hall.'

'Sarcasm does not suit you dear,' she sniffed, and that was another conference down the drain.

Next morning I was doing my exercises on the lawn. It was a beautiful day, and even without my hearing aid, I could make out birds singing. Either that, or my tinnitus was being very innovative. My heart consultant had encouraged me to take up exercise. By which, she meant more than merely lifting a whisky glass a couple of seconds more rapidly than usual to my lips. So, by an immense effort, I managed a trace memory of the torture our old PE instructor put us through during

RAF aircrew training. This was touching the toes and swinging our hips around and of course, running on the spot. I always preferred running on the spot because with normal running you have to come back to where you started after a while. Whereas running on the spot, well it's obvious; you don't go away, so you don't have to return QED.

Anyway, as I fulfilled my quota of energy reserve take-up, I couldn't help noticing a blackbird posing on the branch of our Japanese maple, yes posing. I have never seen a more arrogant creature in my life. It swaggered on the branch like the Laurence Olivier of bird life. It had never occurred to me before, that animals could be snobs, but there was absolutely no mistaking this little creature. Its beak was held up as if there was a nasty smell below. It grandstanded perfectly motionless clearly expecting to be admired for the whole of my six minutes of workout.

I went indoors to tell Sue about this, but as usual, she zapped me with her own experience before I could get a word in. She informed me breathlessly that she had seen four prostitutes down the road. I fetched my glasses, and trotting out immediately to take a look, I completely undid my own theory of running on the spot, as I knew that I would unfortunately, have to come back. All I saw were four of our local blameless sixth formers walking to school. Admittedly, they were not dressed as Sue used to see her own students twenty years ago. These were just the usual seventeen year olds studying A-level harlotry and bondage that Ofsted has brought about with the new national curriculum. The fact is, that I have happy hippy memories of the original miniskirt from swinging

London days. Many a distracted car driver used to end up wrapped around a lamp post. But today's skirts seem to be about three feet shorter than in the 60s. Mind you, my memory, although happy, is not as accurate as it was.

Chapter Three

Eventually you will reach a point when you stop lying about your age and start bragging about it.

I am eighty-five years old this year, but I feel about thirty inside. There was a time when I was always the youngest in the group; at school in the RAF, at work. Eventually, I grew a beard to try to look older than I was. That worked for some years. Well, until the local yobs kept shouting 'Captain Birdseye' after me. Now, when I have the urge to look younger again, shaving off my beard doesn't make it happen. I would look this age under a blanket. What irks me most of all is that if I should try to flirt, like the younger man I feel inside, I get funny looks from women that insinuate that I am not dangerous. I hear whispers that sound like, 'Get lost Granddad,' or at the least, I am convinced that I will eventually hear such mutterings. Why are the old guys, who say the same things at seventy or eighty, that we used to say at thirty or forty, called 'Dirty old men?'

Why, when we were *dirty young men* did no-one mind?

So far in this diatribe you may have thought that I was a grumpy person with the whole world against me. Far from it. I am grateful to be alive, and Susie and I often thank our stars, and our joint pensions, for what we have. Every time an advert comes on the TV for us to help starving children or to dig wells or save the snow leopard; we lurch to our cheque books to sign our names in sheer gratitude for not starving and to have moderately rosy-cheeked offspring. I am supremely grateful that Sue has a wonderful sense of humour. Otherwise, how could she cope with me?

All this reflection about age is because I am thinking of the last time we were in Italy and enquiring about buying a house. It was July and we had both lunched rather well at a beautiful restaurant overlooking the sea in Positano. We decided to visit a local estate agent who advertised that he spoke English.

As soon as we arrived at the office, the salesman looked us over and clearly thought we were badly dressed and too old to take seriously. Well, we are used to that, so persisted and asked if he had any two bedroomed properties in the district. He looked Sue up and down and then turned to me with a superior sneer and said, 'Nothing in your price range.'

This made me pretty angry I can tell you. Our house in England had recently been valued at £740,000 and we had thought of paying at least half that on a place of our dreams and investing the rest for income. So who was this Dago twit assuming we were ancient church mice on holiday. We had already ascertained from the Internet that Italian house prices were quite a bit lower than those in our part of the UK. A two bedroomed house in good nick in Positano was well within our means; as long as we weren't after an historic villa with a cliff edge view.

The agent then compounded his gaffe by saying, 'Surely you are a little too old for the house hunting in this heat?'

So we stormed out and bade the idiot good day. Let him realise all the commission he had missed when he woke up.

We then found another very *benevolo* agent who assumed that we were serious. He sat us both down and offered us each an espresso. I drank mine, but Sue whispered that hers was too strong and in any case she needed to go to the toilet. The *agente immobiliare* finally said he would gladly show us a couple of houses if we came back the next day, as today was his mother's birthday. He also asked if we were interested in sheltered housing, *allogi protetti,* although he was very pleasant about it. As our hotel was a couple of hours away by boat, I said no to the next day, and to the sheltered housing. We went back out into the street. Our spirits were beginning to flag a bit by this time and we needed more refreshment. Sue ordered a huge Coppa Tricolore of ice-cream, and I had a double Grappa.

When we returned to our hotel in Amalfi we were so exhausted we both decided to miss supper and go to bed early.

No more was said the next day and so we returned from yet another holiday with no decision made.

Scarlett phoned this morning. She is changing her job again. I am not surprised; she has never had what you might call a career. She left university with a third in media studies thirty years ago, and then worked in a flower shop for five years. She said it was because at that time, her qualification was new and not understood by employers. Nowadays it is old and understood only too well. If you fail rocket surgery then you do media studies.

She had a big row with the woman who owned the shop (over some mutual friend who got a silver gilt at

Chelsea apparently, I don't know the details) and left to go on the dole for a year before becoming a traffic warden. She seemed to like this and worked at it for quite a while until an angry motorist broke her nose when she gave him a ticket for parking on a double yellow line all night. She tried the Army for two years but that didn't work out either. Since then, I do not really know what she does. She has never met a man she likes. Frankly, it wouldn't surprise me if she became a lesbian. But I doubt if she would stick to that for long. In the meantime she has this new job with an Aids charity in Bethnal Green. She wanted to know if I could direct debit £50 a month to them, as she gets a small percentage of every donation she can bring in. I said absolutely not. We are saving like mad for our new life in Italy. On hearing this, Scarlett went ape and said we were self-centred and only cared about ourselves. I told her that we had supported her and her brother for over thirty extra years, since their childhood, and had been collecting for the lifeboats every summer; and did she realise that her mother had knitted for Nigerian babies for over three years.

This must have struck home, as she put down the phone without saying her usual goodbye.

Sue was out at the hairdressers, so I leapt into the Jag and toddled down to the yacht club to talk things over with Dave Bucknell. It was after twelve noon by the time I arrived, and pouring cats and dogs, so Dave and a couple of others were well away with a comforting smell of single malt in the air.

'Ah here he cometh, Picatho himthelf!' cried my old pal.

'How goeth the move to the Continong   old fruit?'

'Not a chance if my kids have their say,' I replied, 'Mine's a Famous Grouse – double. What's on the lunch menu?'

'What about the houthe? I thought you would have -er- thold it by now?' Dave hiccoughed and lisped, which is quite a feat even after thirty years in the navy.

'We haven't even found somewhere we like in Italy yet. Can't think about selling until we have the buying sorted. At the moment the kids are trying to bleed us dry before we start.'

There were murmurings of consolation all round. Almost everyone in the club had similar experiences with their own offspring. Even Jackie our pretty barmaid-cum-waitress, who can't be more than 25 years old, chipped in saying her six-year-old was blackmailing her for a pair of Nike trainers.

'How can a six -year old do that?' I asked.

'She keeps threatening to find out who her dad is,' said Jackie.

'Well who is he?'

`I dunno do I?' Jackie pulled a pint of lager for the Commodore and plonked it down on the bar with a sullen look.

'Cut them off with a thilling,'said Dave, 'thatth what I did.'

The Commodore, John Wellings, happened to overhear this claim of Dave's and exclaimed, 'You did no such thing Bucknell you old softie. I know for a fact that you coughed up the fares for all three of them to Australia; and you have been sending them remittance money ever since. That's why you had to sell your boat, so no more porkies in the bar if you please.'

John Wellings was Dave's brother-in-law so we knew he was on the ball. Dave tried to laugh it off so I bought him a large gin and tonic. He is a softie, and I like him for it, but that does not solve our little problem.

Scarlett arrived at the house the very next day with her charming friend Jenny. By crikey, if I was five years younger, I'd have a crack at her myself! She is a flaxen haired beauty with a bosom like two rabbits in a sack and hips which seemed to be worked by fluid mechanics. The pair were full of bonhomie and the milk of human kindness. Jenny had brought me some aftershave, which, as I have a beard of some twenty years standing, was thoughtful but perhaps a *touche* impractical. Still, it was kind. Scarlett had brought us both woollen gloves she had knitted herself. These were really to show us that she could not afford a genuine bought present. I know her little games. Nevertheless, I fell on her neck with fatherly gratitude, and told her that they were just what I wanted. This ploy caught her properly on the wrong foot, hooray!

There were a good many family in-jokes and a light lunch thrown together by my indomitable Sue. Then the heavy artillery began. It seems that Beowulf had phoned his sister, after my cruel and heartless refusal to underwrite his carpet cleaning débâcle. He had apparently hinted that I was having delusions and that Alzheimer's might be setting in. This, I explained to my darling daughter, was an amazing coincidence, because the aforesaid last scheme of his seemed to me to smack of the same mental degeneration. The Reader's Digest in my dentist's waiting room had an article all about it; Early Onset Dementia it was called, and her brother had all the symptoms and was in the right age bracket. Did she agree with me? Was she grateful to me for pointing this out? No, how sharper than a serpent's tooth it is to have a thankless child. Yes, I know, I have been reading King Lear to cheer myself up.

Clearly, the mission was not accomplished, and a disgruntled Scarlett returned home. Jenny, on the other hand, seemed mystified by the whole trend of the conversation. I don't blame her. How often is one party to watching a daughter practically accusing her father of being gaga? This, from Scarlett who told us on her last visit, that a strange caller at her flat had asked if he could measure her nose for research purposes, and she had agreed. Two days later a policeman had knocked on the door asking if she had been bothered by a weirdo who was going around with a nasal fetish. Naturally, she was too embarrassed to admit it, but she told her mother, who then gave me the full story between almost unstoppable giggles. She was not assaulted or anything. Apparently, this guy got an immense thrill out of measuring women's noses. (Some mothers do have 'em.)

Later, I rang Beowulf on his mobile and asked him not to go around telling all and sundry that I was a fruit cake. I added that he was pretty demented himself, owning a mobile phone if his income was so low. I had heard that the rent and the calls were far more expensive than our land line. Actually, our own calls are free within the UK, because I got a deal with British Telecom on fast broadband. He apologised at the end of my call, and said that I was not mad, just out-of-date and that was to be expected at my age. So I bit my tongue and bade him goodbye quite civilly.

I don't know any people of my generation who have mobile phones. What on earth would one say to people while out walking? And who wants to be called, or even texted when you are trying to get on with something else? Besides, most of us have arthritic fingers which are too big to hit only one key at a time. Why can't the scientists invent something for old people to communicate with? It would need to have much larger buttons and a louder speaker, weigh much less, and come free with our pensions. Lord knows there are enough of us oldies about now to make it vital. It's called grey power. There are so many of us reaching our 100th birthdays nowadays, that I believe that the poltroons who labour at Buckingham Palace sending out congratulatory cards from the Queen are all developing something called Repetitive Strain Injury as a result of overwork.

Chapter Four

One of the many things no one tells you about ageing is that it is such a nice change from being young.

There is a story that I remember telling my children when they were in their late teens I think. Of course, they might have been younger, or it may be that it was someone else's kids; anyway I forget who it was, but I wanted to make a point. It went like this,

A young bull and an old bull were standing together at the top of a hill and below them in the field they could both see a herd of about twenty cows. The young bull said to his companion, 'Let's race down the hill and shag one of those cows?'

The old bull took a look at the herd and then replied, 'Let's *walk* down the hill and shag the lot of them.'

That's what I call philosophy in a nutshell.

Of course, no-one is considered OLD these days. It's called the 'ageing process'. If you are over 50 you start the ageing process. Soon they offer you free flu jabs, free TV licences and free NHS prescriptions. I dread to think how the drainage/water supply must be swilling around with all the urine/stool samples crammed with so many free chemicals. It wouldn't surprise me one day, if at some innocent sea outlet, say in Dorset or Kent, there was suddenly an enormous explosion caused by a build up of old folks excreting a toxic mix of amitriptyline and syrup of figs. It could make the Japanese tsunami of 2011 look like an ordinary bath plug being pulled out.

The doctors and nurses are all teenagers now anyway and haven't the sense of responsibility they were born with. When I have attended A&E or outpatients they say, 'How are you Peter? Or what would you like for lunch Peter? Bloody cheek! We've not been introduced, and some slip of a girl called a consultant or a nurse practitioner can't be bothered to call me Mr Huntingdon. It's not only disrespectful it's dangerous. I could be some other Peter with only a mild complaint, and not the rather serious Irritable Bowel Syndrome that I suffer. Next thing you know I am labelled Nil by Mouth and robbed of a perfectly good Shepherd's Pie.

You can't tell who are nurses and who are plumbers or electricians these days anyhow. A green jump suit just doesn't hack it for me. When nurses were distinguished by their saucy little caps and black nylons I was usually cured the same day. Just looking at the occasional set of black stockings or the flash of a suspender gave one a lift which could last a week. When I was a young boy, which after all, is not that long ago by NASA standards, doctors were properly dressed; not in scruffy jeans with bomber jackets and hair gel. Our old Dr Agnew-Smythe when I was a boy was a perfect gentleman. He always came to the house in a wing collar and spats. When he sent my mother out to fetch a glass of water, I was quite content for him to undo my trousers. He was very kind and used to call me Master Huntingdon not Peter which I liked a lot. I missed him when he was struck off.

I wish Sue and I were in Italy right now. Unfortunately, we will have to wait until next summer before we can afford another holiday in paradise. We have been to Rome and to Lake Como as well as several other parts where the British have tended to settle, such as Chiantishire and Umbria. Our favourite spot is Ravello, high up on the Amalfi coast. It is a bit cooler than sea level, and it is said that the Roman senators of old used to favour the place. If so, It must have been the climate not the local wine! But the people are friendly and the food terrific. If it was good enough for D.H.Lawrence, Greta Garbo, Virginia Woolf and Gore Vidal, then it's good enough for the Huntingdons. The inhabitants are down-to-earth and friendly. It is a typical Italian family-oriented community. I recall one evening when the local chief of police arrived in the square all peaked cap and jangling medals. He looked like a caricature of Mussolini, very proud, very impressive. Unfortunately, he had his old mother in tow and everywhere they went it was mum who got the respect. Everyone wanted to pat little Benito on the head and tell him how *benissimo* he looked. She kept telling him to blow his nose and sit up straight. It was very very appealing.

Looking on the Internet there are several houses for sale near Ravello, described as home from home with 7 bedrooms and 7 bathrooms for as little as €15,000,000. There is another with 19 bedrooms and 20 bathrooms near Sorrento for €13,000,000. I suppose all those bathrooms means the owners are filthy rich? It is beginning to look as if all we can afford is a small bungalow on the edge of the crater on Vesuvius.

In any case, the whole question of moving house has to be on hold for the next two weeks as it's Wimbledon fortnight, and Sue will be prostrate in front of the 36 inch TV every day unable to move or speak. Thank God I have never taken part in, or watched any kind of sport. Well, I did enjoy a bit of boxing in my young days, but that was because I closed my eyes and attacked the other boxer at rapid speed and with no mercy until he gave up. I never minded being hit. I just wanted to win and get it over. I attribute the fact that I still have my own hips and knees to never playing sport. All my friends that did so, are now staggering about on crutches or in hospital having major joints replaced.

Watching football is to see 22 people, whom you don't know, chase about and fall dramatically every now and again trying to get an Oscar for acting as if they have been foully pole-axed. Cricket is even worse. You have possibly three people out of the 22 getting some exercise, and very slow hand-claps by spectators who aren't watching at all, but chatting to old school friends with whom they once played cricket, or making illegal bets on who is going to chuck a no-ball.

As for Wimbledon, you've either got four people you have never heard of, whacking their racquets about, or two people you've never seen in your life, doing the same. They've brought out some pensioned-off American player who is allowed to be a presenter now that he has promised to stop throwing his racquet at the umpires. For light relief you then have several English players of all three sexes losing, in between bouts of torrential rain. The only decent way to watch Andy Murray is to tune into channel 12 to view re-runs of Auf Wiedersehen Pet and nip over to the centre court for five minutes during the commercials.

It's like watching paint stay wet. As somebody said once, 'For those people who don't have football, there is always religion.'

Mind you, some of the nicest human beings I know are followers of some religion or other, as are some of the nastiest. It is crystal clear to me that gods are invented by people and not the other way around. After all, there are so many gods. We may laugh at the cargo cults of Melanesia, but they are no more amusing to the believers than the Catholic faith to its adherents. When bibles and the book of Mormon first appeared, they were written by men. Only fools can believe that any of this stuff was handed down from some creature we should worship. The Christian Bible and the Koran contain a wealth of knowledge and both good and poor advice; but that is no excuse for leaving one's senses.

Our pets Korky and Jumble have gods; they are Sue and me! They follow us around at times to such an extent that I wish I could send them a plague of frogs. Cats very seldom ask to be taken for walkies; but yesterday when Jumble went nearly mad with his prayers to go for a stroll, Korky joined us and walked down the road to Waitrose like a trained tiger.

Beowulf seems to have forgiven me for being out-of-date and rang me again last night saying he had developed a new interest in horticulture. Well, a sort of hobby really, he said. Whatever next, I thought. It wouldn't have surprised me more if he had told me he was becoming an Avon lady. Neither of our two offspring has ever evinced a concern for gardening; not even growing mustard and cress on a damp flannel. He said he had no room in his apartment (he calls his cramped flat an apartment in a fatuous attempt to sound like a person with an income) to try out some experimental seeds which a friend had brought him from Utrecht. It sounds as if he may have started to develop a healthy enthusiasm for something worthwhile at last. He said he might come down at the weekend if we could spare him a small plot at the back, out of sight. Sue was delighted and raced down to Sainsbury's this morning to buy a chicken. Privately, I thought it was about time that our eldest brought us a pheasant and some champagne when he visited, but said nothing. I was annoyed that she chose Sainsbury's because I have boycotted the place ever since they went for orange as their corporate colour scheme. Orange is such bad taste. For the same reason I could never bring myself to fly on an Easyjet plane.

Anyway, some amazing news has pushed these minor concerns right out of the window! I had a letter in the post today from a publisher saying that he was interested in reissuing my old book on body art, and someone called Simon Postlethwaite asked if the rights had reverted to me? Well of course they had never left me. The first issue sold less than ten copies, seven of which were to me personally. Even the libraries had never taken it up. Now it seems, 'The New Art' is to be re-published under the title '1970's Art: Was it Real?' I have written back giving my permission for the go-ahead and have been promised a 7% royalty on sales.

I shan't hold my breath though; but on the other hand we might be able to buy a little villa situated a bit lower down the slope from the actual crater. I told Sue to buy one of those bottles of Chianti covered in straw that we used to make lamps out of, to go with the chicken.

I told Dave Bucknell about the new publication of the book when I drove down to the club for lunch the following day. He was suitably impressed, and before I could stop him had called for a bottle of champers from Jackie the barmaid. We were eating sausage and mash at the time and it didn't really seem appropriate, as I whispered to Dave. He just laughed aloud and slapped me on the back.

'Nonthenthe old thport! It'th not often we have a real live author in the club,' he chortled.

Then several others gathered round and one thing led to another, and we all ended up getting pretty sozzled. If I ever have any royalties coming, I must have spent most of them that afternoon. The chaps all seemed to think I was going to be famous, and indeed, after a few jars, I was inclined that way myself.

Beowulf turned up late on Sunday morning. That is, after lunch, which finishes with us at about two o'clock. Sue brought out the charred half of chicken and some spinach and potatoes that had dried up completely in the bottom oven of the Aga. Beowulf took one look and asked if we had any beer. Fortunately, I had brought several bottles of Heinekens at the club, before driving home completely under the influence, but of course, not a copper in sight in this part of Hampshire; so I got away with it again. I think it's disgraceful, I could have killed somebody.

'What's this interest in horticulture all of a sudden son?' I asked, when he had downed a couple of medium-sized bottles. 'Leave it Pops. I've had a hard day' he said, and slumped into my favourite chair to watch the football. I nearly said *pardon me for breathing* but decided to be patient with him instead.

Last night I had the old dream again. It must be twenty years since I last had it so I suppose I can't complain. I was in my battle position in the Lancaster. It was pitch dark and the flak was bursting all around making huge white flashes inside the aircraft as well as on the clouds outside. I was fixated to the bomb sight looking down as we floated across the enemy landscape. I was terrified as always, having thrown up into a paper bag twelve times on our last twelve missions, but had confidence in my pilot, Merv. He was a calm and unflappable Aussie. I could see long white curving shapes crossing and re-crossing like spaghetti below. We were over Italy, which is strange, because I only ever went on ops over Germany. Wait, the shapes below us *were* spaghetti. All I could see was a river of ravioli, paths of perciatelli. Now we were over the crater of that most unstable volcano, mount Vesuvius. I started to fall through the bomb sight towards the fiery crater... I woke up just in time to realise that I was in my own bed beside Sue.

I used only to have this dream when I had on my mind some impending doom. I wonder what it could be this time?

My eldest boy planted his experimental seeds in a corner of the garden and left to take the bus back to Reading. I noticed that he took the four remaining bottles of lager with him.

Chapter Five

Good judgement comes from experience, and a lot of that comes from bad judgement.

Acting quite out of character this morning, I treated myself to a cappuccino in Starbucks, cost £2.15. As I sat drinking it, I realised that I had paid more than my whole term's pocket money for it, when I was at school in the 1930s. There were 240 pence to the pound then, and I had one pound ten shillings per term. My favourite iced bun was three pence at the tuck shop. Thus I had enough money to buy 120 buns during a ten week term; that could have been 12 buns a week! Of course, I needed to spend money on other things. A cinema seat was twelve pence, equivalent to four buns! But the cappuccino this morning cost more than my term's pocket money. Of course that was in the olden days before police officers drove about in *Skodas* and 70 year old grannies walked the streets in tight jeans.

So what about inflation in general? In those days you could buy a bungalow for £500. Today, the cheapest two bedroom bungalow in Hampshire would be about £100,000, that is 200 times higher. A pair of trousers back then would have cost roughly £1, but this morning I saw trousers for £16. So some clothing has gone up by 16 times, but houses by 200 times. The lesson there is to invest in property not pantaloons.

Saint Pantaleone is the patron saint of Ravello. Even the thought of trousers brings me back to the place.

All this mental activity has been brought about by my obsession with moving to southern Italy. We like Naples, but to visit occasionally not to live there. We remember that there are times when the rubbish is not collected, and the Mafia starts getting involved. (I know that is much the same in England with the Conservative party) but we like the coast rather than the city; so Naples itself is out.

Ravello is over 4,000 feet above sea level at its highest point, and an old legend has it that when the Devil took Christ up to a high spot to tempt him with the beauty of the earth, it was Ravello that he chose.

When I retired from teaching, I thought I would never do any more art again. Nevertheless, after a year or so, I got a bit bored and began to make a few small watercolours. As our friends seem to like them, I started doing more and giving them away. It was a relief not to be teaching snotty-nosed teenagers but to be drawing and painting entirely for myself. I took the plunge, loosened up, and created more abstract pictures. I introduced bits of crinkly paper and silver paint, and instead of our friends saying 'That's nice Peter', they began to say 'What is it?'

That's when I grew the beard. Dave Bucknell was hugely amused. He said that a handlebar moustache was OK for an ex crab-fat like myself, but that I had to have served two years before the mast before growing a beard. I said that I felt sure I could sell paintings if I looked the part and that it was not only sailors that grew beards.

'That ith true,' he answered, 'I have theen a couple of ladieth in the thircus with a dethent set of whithkerth, but I am thure they were ex wrenth anyway'.

I approached several local galleries with samples of my work but none of them showed any interest. One man said he might put a couple up for a week or so on sale or return. I accepted immediately. Then a week later he phoned me and asked me to collect them as they were giving his business a bad name. A stroppy customer had actually asked how much would he pay him to take them away?

I never had the courage to take the advice of Norman Rockwell, which was, that if a painting wasn't going very well, put a puppy in it, a mongrel, never one of the full-bred puppies and then put a bandage on its foot!

I then had this idea of putting Korky to sleep, slicing her in halves and suspending the bits in a glass tank of formaldehyde, but the gallery owner chappie said it had all been done before. So another idea of building up a reasonable bank balance towards our Italian house was knocked on the head.

This morning Sue and I had a profound, almost numinous conversation, concerning our marriage. This sort of thing doesn't happen very often and so I treasure it when it does. I asked if she remembered vowing to honour and obey me and she said she did. Whereupon I asked why was it that I was always going downstairs to get her tea in the mornings? She responded to remind me that I had promised to worship her with my body and that I used my body to fetch the tea; QED.

I also decided to count my farts today as there was a thoughtful documentary on TV about the function of the human body. Apparently, we all let off an average of 14 farts per day, even the queen is not exempt. I thought it important to check this out to see if it was fact or fiction. By 9.10 am I had counted up to 6. Heaven knows what my average will be by bed time. As it turned out, I only counted two more until bed time making me six below the average.

***

Dave Bucknell has invited me to come sailing with him for a week on the Solent. We are to charter a 32 foot bilge-keel yacht called *Thistledo,* and start out from the marina near Portsmouth. No plans but just to swan around between Hampshire and the Isle of Wight. Dave is a qualified yacht-master, and anyway was in the Navy for years and so I feel quite safe on the water with him as long as we don't have a storm. We have been out for a few weekends over the years, but never for a whole week. I asked Sue what she thought of the idea and she said, 'Go for goodness sake. I shall be glad to be rid of you for a few days. You can both get drunk every night and seduce all the girls that will have you...' Then she burst out into uncontrollable laughter; I really have no idea why. I left her still giggling her heart out and drove down to the club to tell Dave the good news. When I told him about her uncontrolled merriment, he was as mystified as I was.

After a long pause, he said 'How many girlth do you think would have uth?' I refused to take him seriously and did not reply.

We started off from Port Solent in fine fettle by ten o'clock in the morning. Dave had made a huge fruit cake, he was good at that, and Sue had packed us ham sandwiches for the first day. Dave had thoughtfully brought a litre bottle of Famous Grouse. We tend to use Italian restaurants as way points when sailing, so no cooking on board required. Being a bit stiff in the joints I always sit down and steer, while Dave, who is pretty natty and swift in his pink canvas sailing trousers and RNSA Breton cap, pulls all the strings and adjusts the sails. Besides, he is three years younger than I am. Most of the time we run under engine and jib. After about fifty minutes we were abreast the Spinnaker tower and heading for the Solent itself when the first mishap occurred. I felt a nasty bump, and although we were in fairly deep water, the boat came to a standstill. The engine stopped and would not re-start. We were in one of the narrowest and busiest parts of Portsmouth harbour and drifting out on the tide. Dave looked over the stern and proclaimed at the top of his voice,

'Plathtic bag!'

I peered over the pushpit too and saw a giant piece of plastic. It looked like one of those transparent covers for a double mattress. One half of it was under the boat, presumably wound around the prop.

'What do we do?' I asked feebly.

'I'll call the harbour-mathter,' said Dave who leapt onto the VHF radio like a cat on a mouse and described our predicament. He had some difficulty, as the harbour master had to keep asking him to repeat anything that had an 's' or a 'c' in it. Dave kept saying 'Plathtic, P-L-A-ETH-T- I -THEE' and the patient guy on the other end kept saying. 'Please speak in English.'

Meanwhile, we were gradually drifting out of the harbour mouth and becoming a hazard to shipping. Two large ferries needed to move out of the way of our track, and I distinctly saw the captain of one of them waving his fist and shouting as he chugged past. After about half-an-hour two men of the harbour staff arrived in a fibre-glass dory covered in multicoloured paint splashes. One of them had a mask and flippers and a huge carving knife. Within five minutes he had dived under our boat and popped up triumphantly holding the tattered remains of the plastic bag. He shouted to us that we could start the motor again, which I did. I called out 'What do we owe you?' But he laughed and waved us away, which we thought was very generous.

Outside the harbour the wind freshened to a force five and the sea began to build up; short choppy waves with an occasional breaker over the bow. Dave reeled in the roller jib and we continued under engine power only. It was wet and difficult but not dangerous, although I did say no when Dave offered me one of Sue's sandwiches. We had decided to lunch at Wootton Creek. There is a double tide in the Solent so we only had 6 hours instead of the conventional 12 hours of tidal help.

Wootton Creek is on the Island (as we nautical types call the Isle of Wight) and is only approachable for about two hours around one of the high tides. Under engine, and with a fairly strong wind we were able to make around five knots. It took a rather stomach-churning hour and a half before we were able to anchor up the creek. We then took the inflatable ashore to the Fishbourne pub for a meal.

Two curries, two black forest gateaux and two bottles of Rioja later, it was four pm when we were asked to leave the pub. I was absolutely fine, but Dave was much the worse for wear. I could tell that because he looked all blurred. It took us half an hour to find the inflatable because I swear someone had moved it. Then we discovered that the tide had gone out and the yacht had settled happily in the mud perfectly upright on its twin keels, only twenty-five yards from the shore. Anyhow, the bottom looked firm to me and I suggested that we just drag the inflatable behind us and walk out to the vessel. It seemed a jolly good idea at the time and we laughed quite a bit when we each saw how splashed with sludge the other had become. Finally, when the brown ooze had come up over our wellies and we were only half way to the yacht, it did not seem so amusing. We were both stuck. It felt like Scott of the Antarctic only brown instead of white!

'We had better call for help,' said Dave. So we turned painfully towards the shore and I fell over, luckily straight into the inflatable. We waved our arms about and called 'Help' until some small children spotted us, and one evidently ran to find his dad. Two rather pale and weedy looking fishermen in huge thigh boots then came and stared at us for a while, assessing our predicament we hoped. Then we saw them pulling some planks of wood down the bit of beach and onto the mud towards us. Gradually, they made a sort of causeway by walking on one plank while carrying another and reached us.(It looked very like the officer selection course we had to pass in the RAF in 1940). They made Dave get into the inflatable as well, and then dragged us both back to the dry land.

They offered to hose us down which we accepted; then it was back to the pub to buy both lads a drink. It was not open of course, but one of them was the landlord's brother-in-law and so the bar was put at our disposal. We stayed there with our new friends Kevin and Wayne until the tide came in at around eight o'clock. Then with much merriment and alcohol fuelled bravado, we were launched in the dinghy and we rowed out to the yacht and clambered aboard. By this time, the ham sandwiches, although dry, seemed heaven sent and we turned in contented and snored our way into oblivion.

The following morning 6.00 am found us surrounded by thick fog. Even the shore was not visible, so we decided to sleep on for another couple of hours. We woke again as if by mutual consent at ten thirty. The tide was well in and the sun shone brightly. Dave planned to sail to Cowes and so made ready with the jib up and the engine turned on. There was a battery driven anchor winch controlled by a hand held remote.

Dave went forward to work it and I stayed on the wheel and in control of the engine. After a small delay up forrard, Dave shouted, 'It'th thtuck, the anchor won't budge.' So I switched off the engine and went up to have a look. After trying it several times it became clear that the anchor was well and truly caught. Dave and I looked at one another and spoke simultaneously,

'Kevin and Wayne!'

Ten minutes of frantic paddling back to the shore to find our rescuers resulted in success, thank goodness! Kevin turned up with a snorkel mask and flippers, which we now realise must be the most important emergency kit in any decent yacht. He dived down to the anchor for what seemed about fifteen minutes, and popped up again gasping with the cold.

'You've got your CQR (another sailing shorthand for a particular anchor; CQR = secure, get it?) dragged right under a submersed cable' he finally spat out, treading water and looking fairly exhausted. Of the two men, he was the more weedy. In fact he was lightly draped in seaweed as we watched.

'I think I can fix it though, but I need a spade.'

Kevin then swam back and trudged up the little beach watched by a small crowd of his friends. One of them fetched a garden spade and handed it over. Kevin then swam back to us waiting in *Thistledo*, hung on the anchor chain to catch his breath for a moment then dived down with the spade. He must have beaten the world record for holding his breath and I was just about to jump over the side to attempt a fruitless rescue when he came up, spade in hand, and shouted, 'You're free!' Dave had realised this fact a minute earlier, as we were floating and dragging our anchor slowly towards the mouth of the creek. He pressed the right button on the remote and the anchor came up. In the meantime, I had the presence of mind to reach down and turn on the diesel which started immediately. Unfortunately, by this time we were a hundred yards downstream and floating into the Solent. It was too far away to thank Kevin for exhausting himself, so we waved joyfully and gave him thumbs up signs which he may or may not have seen and set course for Cowes.

Apart from running aground off Lepe, just west of the Beaulieu river-mouth, and having to be pulled off by a shallow draught gin palace that kindly came to our rescue; no further incidents marred our week's sailing.

Chapter Six

I don't know how I got over the hill without getting to the top.

Sue and I first began to visit Campania sometime during the seventies. Scarlett and Beowulf were around ten and twelve years old, and though I say it myself, were quite delightful children. We could not afford to fly or to stay in hotels. We drove our elderly Volkswagen van and pitched our tent in camp-sites along the way. The smell of wild flowers was everywhere in those summers. Our travels since, locked into a British Airways aluminium tube and picked up by taxis, have never matched that time.

We always took the ferry to France and drove lazily through the sunny countryside and stopping where it looked interesting. I will never forget coming out of our tent one morning and seeing a Frenchman yawning and stretching and calling to his wife, 'Il fait froid.' It was the first time I appreciated that what we had learnt in school was a real language!

We ate frog's legs, which the children said looked like little people, and snails which they both relished. We learnt about French cheeses and, of course, French bread. It seemed a much more free and easy time in those far off days. Sue was beautiful and attracted a lot of attention from Lotharios even in the smallest villages. I once had to threaten to punch one of them on the nose until he left her alone. That was the nearest I have ever come to physical violence in my adult life.

Our drive took us through Switzerland where the mountains were more beautiful than the people. Did I say more beautiful? I really meant more interesting. It was raining one weekend and we thought we would take the kids to a movie. No children allowed in the cinema on a Sunday. At least we didn't have to eat frog's legs.

Arriving in Italy, it was as if the waters of Lago Maggiore had cleansed out the cold puritan penny-pinching experience of the Swiss and warmed us to the heart. There is nothing like the Italians to wipe out the disappointing experience of most other European nations. We fell in love with the country immediately. The first shop that we went into, we didn't have enough lira to pay for the produce we chose. The shopkeeper just waved us away and said 'Is OK, come back tomorrow.' No-one within a 100 mile radius of Zurich had ever said anything so easygoing to us. So naturally, we were on their doorstep first thing in the morning.

Now it was our turn to discover more about Italian dishes. I have always loved spaghetti bolognese as it has a bit more meat about it than much other pasta. But we experienced real pizza (as opposed to pizza with pineapple on it!), risotto, tortellini, and toppings of delicious *parmigiana*. We found out how often an Italian restaurant owner will greet you like a long lost relative if you return within a few days. Also, I personally was fascinated to find out that the big sunglasses that make young women look so glamorous in Italy usually revealed tiny piggy eyes when they were removed. Of course, the girls who don't wear sunglasses are stunning.

***

This morning I had a fantastic surprise. An envelope arrived with a cheque for £840 from the new publishers of my book '1970's Art Was it Real'. It seems that they have sold 1000 copies at £12 each. There was a letter from Simon Postlethwaite saying that he expected to sell many more as there was an interest among certain American universities. It may be put on their official reading lists. I immediately rang back to ask him which universities, but his secretary, after a long pause and some talking in the background, said he was out to lunch. This at ten o'clock in the morning. I am amazed at how some jobs allow such louche behaviour. How does he get any work done? I shall certainly ring again when he is in the office.

If the sales continue like this we shall have a real chance of real estate in Ravello. Get it? A real chance? Oh well, please yourself.

By the same post there was a letter from the old boys society from my school inviting me to a re-union dinner in London at a mere £65 per head. Of course, it's an old *girls* and boys nostalgia society now, and naturally run totally and firmly by the more recently accepted women. After 70 odd years I had thought that my connection with the place was decently dead and buried. In fact, for many years it was. I have always looked with great suspicion at those people who cling on to their old school and never seem to leave. Some, who are evidently stuck into a permanent adolescence, even return to live in the same town as their alma mater. Of course, since the invention of Google and women, ancient links and addresses have been resurrected, and goodness knows how many dark secrets have been blown from placid lives. I am certainly not going to any sort of reunion, and will write back in a disguised hand saying I have deceased, and that neither have I left them anything in my will. Damned cheek of them to suggest it. They can have all my homesick tears and the twisted ankle I got from skipping out of the way of a fast ball on the cricket boundary if they want a contribution.

Where was I? Ah yes, memories of happier days in Italy. One of my great disappointments in those otherwise very happy days was the quality of Italian wine. It hasn't improved much either. There was quite a scandal in the 1980s concerning the addition of antifreeze to Italian wines. I could have told them about that ten years earlier during the 1970s. There was a great deal of talk at that time about a huge wine lake in Italy. I have no idea where it was situated, but I could imaging great truckloads of antifreeze being driven to the lake edge by half -shaven spaghetti-eating viticulturists and tipped in with gleeful expressions and poorly rendered guttural snatches from Puccini. We always tried the local wines wherever we stopped for a snack and were forever disappointed. Some were just like bottled water such as Frascati, supposed to be made from Malvasia biance di Candia grapes, and the favourite wine of Pope Gregori XVI. Other local tipples were more like gasoline, you could light bonfires with them. If you are prepared to pay a small fortune for a Barolo or Barbaresco or Brunello, then you might have a decent drink that will put hairs on your chest, but it will cost you more than ordinary French or German wine. Just remember, in Italy, order wine that begins with the letter B and there is a fair chance that it may not be lighter fluid.

The first bottle of wine I ever remember was in Sicily. It was a lovely light green orb wrapped in straw or raffia containing red Chianti and I was enchanted with it. There was a time during the fifties when you did not buy a bottle of wine unless you could make a lampstand out of it later. Wine was never part of our life in post-war Britain. Apart from sherry at Christmas, which was obligatory, you would have to be very upper-middle to drink wine during the rest of the year. I don't remember what that Chianti tasted like now, but two of us had ordered a pizza, also the first we had ever tasted, and the wine came with it quite naturally. Of course, in Italy, food and wine go together like bacon and eggs or snakes and ladders or Laurel and Hardy; all of those pairs of mere words which trip evenly off the tongue, and there is a reason for it. The Italians have spent thousands of years finding out what goes with what in food and drink, so trying to find a new combination is impossible because it has all evolved over generations.

Years later, having gone through the ways of most young English wine bibbers, Chianti, Beaujolais, Blue Nun, Mattheus Rose, Sauterne, I realised that the very act of opening the bottle, pulling the cork was a large part of the enjoyment. Wine drinking is usually a companionable act. I know that plenty of people like a glass or two on their own, but that is not exactly what wine was made for.

Wine drinking alcoholics are doubly sad people. They miss out on seventy-five percent of the whole point, which is appreciation, companionship and of course, making the lampstands. Getting out one's favourite corkscrew and grasping the bottle with a couple of friends looking on in anticipation gives an edge to the occasion.

When my father presented me with a dusty and rather deranged looking bottle of 1956 Doudet Naudin Burgundy sometime during the late sixties, I was delighted. He told me it would keep for another fifty years and possibly quadruple in value. He knew nothing about wine, well perhaps rather more than I did, but his friend the wine merchant in Exeter had sold him six bottles and he had passed this one on to me. We had no cellar in those days, as a lowly school teacher, so I put it in the back of my garage, and almost forgot about it. Nevertheless, it got me much more interested in wine than I had been before.

I even attempted briefly to learn Spanish on the back of this interest in viniculture. This resulted in my now historic attempt to order a particular wine, using my fledgling Spanish, in a restaurant in Marbella, which caused the puzzled waiter to bring me a fried egg resting on a lettuce leaf. A couple of decades later, Beowulf told this story to a Spanish friend, who laughed until the tears came, because, he said, there really is a Spanish wine whose name sounds very like a fried egg on lettuce. What a pity my grasp of the Spanish tongue is so tentative that I am unable to verify this.

All this time I would now and again think about my father's gift of the Doudet Naudin 1956 and look forward to the day when we would find an occasion great enough to celebrate and open it.

We moved house to follow my promotion and the bottle moved with us. I made sure it was looked after properly and we wrapped it in a towel and took it with us in the car. It was not an artefact to be entrusted to ham-handed removal men, well known for dropping grand pianos and smashing crystal decanters.

Next in my saga of wine drinking came the holidays to Greece. Greece for my family will always be associated with sailing. I doubt whether we have ever penetrated further inland than two kilometres anywhere in Greece as we have always been on a boat. Thus our drinking has been in small tavernas and never in posh restaurants. Consequently, the wine has been either Retsina or similar and local. Well, a palate brainwashed by Rioja and the Bulgarian Cabernet of the 1970s is not going to enjoy any bucolic Greek vino. To add injury to insult, by ordering a dusty bottle of French wine, which had been on the shelf in a Greek taverna gently sautéed in the sun of three or four seasons, invited severe disappointment. We may have been ignorant wine snobs, but even then we could smell a corked and cooked Bordeaux at fifty paces. So, perhaps impetuously we decided against Greek wines. It is the only country whose wines I have never looked for in an English supermarket. I once hosted an afternoon of the U3A wine tasting class, and ordered six bottles of Greek wine in order to challenge the group. It was the first session where the members asked for a bucket to spit out the tiny samples!

Holidays in Italy however were not so bad. In the rolling hills of Tuscany we experienced our old favourites of Chianti and Orvieto and reluctantly left the potential lampstands behind due to baggage restrictions on British Airways. But our growing taste buds were finding these wines a bit, well, tinny. The Barolo was more satisfying. As for the Italian white wines, I was yet to discover the summer delight of Pinot Grigio, but had learned enough to realised that Frascati was probably just distilled water in a white bottle.

On our fiftieth wedding anniversary I opened the 1956 Doudet Naudin with a flourish using my favourite corkscrew. It smelled like an opened drain and tasted like vinegar that had been through a cat. Who knows, without the stimulus of that bottle squatting patiently in our garage, we might never have had learnt enough to have the confidence to pour its contents down the sink.

Anyway, I hastened to find my Sue to tell her about the cheque from Postlethwaite, but discovered that she had gone to an early choir practice or perhaps some lecture on gardenias. I never know what enthusiasm she has from day to day. I find it hard enough myself to concentrate on what pills to take with my breakfast. So I got in the Jag and wheeled down to the high street to see my personal banker Charlotte and to pay in the cheque. By the time I had parked and found my way to the Midland, difficult, since it is now called the HSBC, Charlotte had been replaced by a goofy nerd about nine feet tall with bottle- bottom glasses called Omar Mohammed. He is the fifth personal banker I have been given since the manager died and was never replaced.

I have never actually met any of these special creatures more than once before they are superseded. It all seems extremely *impersonal* to me. But then, years ago, I used to have a manager who gave me sherry and wrote with a quill. Omar received my cheque with what seemed indecent alacrity, and then tried to sell me insurance. I told him that I had had full insurance for everything, ever since I flew in Lancasters with the son of the Managing Director of the Prudential. (He was our rear gunner with an amazingly good aim.) Omar sighed as he obviously saw another commission biting the dust. But as I told him, I don't come into the bank seeking a protection racket. I just want to pay in some cheques and then take out some spending money occasionally, QED.

On my return to *chez nous,* or I suppose I should say *cosa nostra,* in preparation for our proposed change of nationality; I found an empty house and no sign of my beloved. After I had made myself a cheese sandwich and a small glass of the Times Wine Club Barolo, and sat down to watch Bargain Hunt on the telly, the phone rang. It was Sue, ringing from our daughter's home in Battersea. Her first words were 'Have you had anything to eat?' I assured her that culinarily speaking I was hunky dory. She then said that she had been asked to stay by Scarlett who was very upset about something, (I suspected a woman's problem immediately, always on safe ground there) and could I look after myself for a day or two. Of course I said yes and asked what the problem was. 'I can't speak now – tell you more when I get home.' she said in a low voice. So I said toodle-pip and mum's the word and so on, and put down the phone.

This was a perfect opportunity to call old Dave Bucknell and suggest we meet for dinner in our favourite hostelry, the Plough at Sparsholt. So later, after the famed liver and bacon followed by a fine apple crumble, we chatted in our usual amicable way, each with a large brandy in hand.

'Tho Thcarlett is going through the change do you think?' he asked gravely.

I replied that I did not think so. She was hardly out of nappies as far as I was concerned.

'Do lethbians have the menopauthe like other women?' he asked.

I was outraged and amazed. 'Who said Scarlett was a lesbian?' I demanded. 'What on earth makes you say that?'

'Thorry, I thought everybody knew. Ethpethially you of all people. You are her father. What about that thtunning partner of herth, Jenny?' Then it dawned on me what he was telling me. Scarlett was gay. It all made sense now. I had always thought that *partner* meant they were *in* business together, not doing the business.

'I realithed Jenny wath gay when I tried to kith her one time at your Chrithmath party.' said Dave looking rather mournful.

'She always kisses me. No problem.' I retorted.

'Yeth but you are her father-in-law tho to thpeak; family.'

Once more I was flabbergasted to realise the truth of old Dave's point. We parted outside in the car park in quiet mood.

I drove carefully home and sat glumly in front of the TV without noticing what was playing. An advert came on loudly proclaiming the benefit of some mouth ulcer jelly which I found mildly distasteful. This was followed by another assault on my sensitivities advertising panty liners, whatever they might be. Then it was all about fungal infections followed by a new offer on sanitary towels. Next, I was battered by an unsavoury presentation about vaginal sprays. Even putting my fingers in my ears, closing my eyes, and chanting 'Da da da di da' loudly, did nothing to erase the images.

I grabbed the remote, killed the transmission and stumbled whimpering upstairs to bed. The nightmares that followed were a relief from the embarrassments of TV advertising.

Chapter Seven

There are three kinds of men: The ones that learn by reading. The few who learn by observation. The rest of them have to pee on the electric fence and find out for themselves.

Sue arrived home at coffee time looking pale, and frankly, uninteresting. There is no more dismal sight than an octogenarian wife who has had a hard time with her daughter.

I gave her the obligatory hug and a mug of de-caf to settle her down. 'It's OK dear,' I said as re-assuringly as I could manage, 'I understand what you have been going through. It was a shock to me too. But we must just be *contemporaneo* about it.' 'What do you mean?' she said. 'I haven't told you what's happened yet.'

'I think I am mature enough to accept the situation.' I said, in a kindly way. I ventured to put my arm around Sue's shoulders and give her a chummy hug. But she shrugged me off, a bit irritably, I thought.

'What are you talking about?' she asked; with what I can only describe as a pert look, not too attractive in a pensioner.

'I am well aware that Scarlett is a gay person,' I said.

'Well I think we have known that for some years now dear.' She had instantly turned from pert to patronising. It was not a pretty sight. She continued, 'Scarlett is having a baby.'

'Who's the father?' I asked. It was a knee jerk question.

'Some sperm donor, we don't know his name. They are anonymous you know?'

'She can't be pregnant; she's too old.' That, at least, I was sure of.

'Don't be ridiculous Peter. Jenny is actually having the baby. She's only 35. We're going to be grandparents at last.'

I gave this a few moments of what was for me complex thought before further comment, and then it struck me like a sack of melons on the head, 'Yes, but we shall be completely unrelated to our grandchild though.'

Our conversation then continued all through lunch and for most of the afternoon. I don't think we had had such an interesting chat since my mother died suddenly doing press-ups in the gym at 91 years old.

Later that evening Sue rang Beowulf and gave him the glad tidings that he was to be an uncle. He seemed particularly unconcerned as he said that he too was about to make an announcement. He had a new girlfriend who was *THE ONE*. She was an antique dealer in Reading. When pressed for more details by Sue, it turned out that she actually attended a lot of car boot sales and did a bit of house clearance when she could. Beowulf has been helping her out with various items from the corporation tip where he works. Her name is Magda and she is expecting a baby too; from her previous partner, some Romanian dentist.

'So now we are suddenly expecting two grandchildren who are both entirely unrelated to us by race, creed, blood or DNA,' I cried peevishly. 'If there was ever a cynical plot to put a stop to our moving abroad, this is it!'.

I stomped off into my study, which is really the spare bedroom with an ancient school desk reclaimed from a skip, and an old laptop. It was decorated in a chintzy way many years ago and is one of those cosy environments where one feels safe. I play the mouth organ in there to cheer myself up, and occasionally listen to jazz on a small portable CD player.

After a decorous interval, Sue knocked on the door and called out 'Would you like a cup of filthy tea?' I still get caught out by her strange statements, but it turned out that she said 'milky tea'. I do wish she would speak up when talking through doors.

***

The next day I had to go to the local hospital for a long-standing appointment to have a CT scan. No breakfast, and I had to drink at least a litre of clear water an hour before. I drove to the department in the

Jag and paid two hours in advance for a place in the packed hospital car park. Once inside, I was whisked away by an incredibly pot-bellied nurse labelled Moyra, A truly poor example of diet for a representative of the medical profession. I was given a strange garment like a ripped nightgown into which I was left to struggle. There was a single hole which I naturally assumed was for my head. However, I then became the object of uproarious laughter from all and sundry when I stood uncomfortably with bare arms and my bum flapping in the breeze. It seemed that I had been given a garment with one arm cut off, especially made for one-armed patients. I had forced my head through the arm hole. After this was sorted out I became, as it were, a child or a pet of some sort. Moyra adopted me and kept saying sentences like 'Peter, would you lie down here *for me?*' and 'Now Peter hold your left arm out *for me?*' It was like being in kindergarten. I wasn't there for *her* I was there entirely for me. Then it took chubby Moyra an incredible time to discover a vein to inject with iodine. She kept muttering 'Do you have any veins darling?' and 'Don't worry sweetheart we'll find one eventually.' I am a passionate admirer and support of the National Health Service which has kept me and mine alive and kicking for free since world War Two; but some of the nurses need re-training in how to deal with senior citizens. I said nothing out of respect for her vocation, but a pithy email to the editor of the Radio Times will soon be on its way.

Finally, the huge doughnut which was the scanner, swallowed me whole and asked me in a comforting dalek voice to hold my breath for 6 seconds then to breathe normally. Thank God it did not say 'Hold your breath for *me...*'

I was back in the car park in under 50 minutes having paid for an extra hour and ten minutes that I did not need. Altogether, I was not best pleased with the medical experience and only hope that I have a serious disease to make the whole thing worthwhile.

Returning home I had to consider the family once more, and try to make sense of our weird offspring, their life choices and motivation. Scarlett and Jenny were a surprise to me, but after my friends and I broke all the rules in the sixties, I suppose I should have expected lifestyles to change forever. Beowulf has just failed to grow up and to take responsibility for himself. I can't see him making a serious go of it with this new girl of his. Whenever I have ventured a mild criticism of either of either of our two in the past, Beowulf just chuckles and says,

'I blame the parents'.

There is, of course, no answer to that.

Sue has gone to stay with an old school friend in Norfolk. I encourage this as it gives her and her chum Cynthia a chance to remember their past glories in the school lacrosse team and bullying the first years when they were prefects. They usually go out for a drink and a meal in the local pub and eye all the beautiful young men from the air base nearby. Being invisible old ladies makes it a very easy pastime apparently. In their flower-power youth with their micro mini-skirts and uninhibited attitudes, they were something to be reckoned with. The young men they are watching now have no idea what is going through the heads of two old girls sipping gin and tonic in the corner.

Meantime, I am able to relax in our home and get used to being on my own and eating and drinking what I like. I don't shower or clean my teeth. I chuck Korky and Jumble out for good and lock all the doors. I then take enormous pleasure in leaving the lavatory seat up permanently. In the evening I lie on the sofa in front of the TV in my pyjamas at 7 o'clock, with a large single malt and a pizza, watching a western that I had previously recorded for this purpose.

The following morning I wallowed in bed for an extra two hours. I had almost woken from an titillating dream in which I was enjoying having a close relationship of the 'nooky' variety with Jackie the barmaid from the yacht club. She was a lovely girl in my dream, rather more willing and voluptuous in that capacity than in real life. It is a mystery what characters dreams furnish us for entertainment or even horror. I accept that it is probably out of our conscious control. Sue has always maintained that we cannot help our dreams and so we occasionally share such bawdy night time experiences with one another in a relaxed way. However, I am not sure that I can be excused from *deliberately prolonging* this particular reverie once I realised that I was almost awake, and forced myself back into sleep and that erotic mental picture again.

It is only the pathetic whining and scratching of the animals that brings me spiralling down to earth. So I have to go wearily downstairs and under the furious eyes of Korky and the ecstatic tail wagging of Jumble, put out their various dishes. Once again, I cut my thumb on the whale-meat and turnip dog food tin, and splash my pyjamas with the obscene sachet of Korky's exotic beaver and millet puree. Why they both can't catch and eat the rats which experts tell us are no more than 15 feet away from us in any direction, I don't know. Actually, Korky did catch a rat once and brought it into the kitchen, laid it down on the new cork floor and looked up expecting to win the Nobel prize or something. Sue had to pick the unfortunate rodent up by the tail wearing Daffodil gloves (Sue, not the rat) and put it into the dustbin.

Beo dropped in for ten minutes today. I noticed that he had shaved his head, I suppose to disguise the fact that his hair has started to recede. I have always been fascinated by his hair styles over the years. When he was about eighteen he had flowing locks and looked like a re-incarnation of Charles II. Of course hair has been a constant source of the most wonderful social divisions for many years, possibly for centuries. This is a minefield for men rather than women, because women of all classes have always been able to experiment with their hair. Men in England have never been so fortunate in modern times. Almost any departure from the demob haircut since 1945 has incurred the wrath or discomfort of somebody. The sporting of a teddy boy DA or of hippy long hair, Jamaican dreadlocks or the shaven hard man type, has never given any advantage to the wearer in this society. It has long been a truism that any extreme departure, from the norm of short back and sides, has resulted in in a young man becoming a laughing stock . In England, the home of inverted snobbery, where this loss of social standing is often the very reason for adopting weird styles, it can be assumed that some nutty political statement is the cause. The subsequent addition of nose, eyebrow and ear rings, with piercings of every kind, will force the wearer to take up a potent aggressive stance to gain any sort of status. Naturally Beowulf used such unattractive fashions to fight against social norms anyway for years. There are so many insidious prejudices against short hair, long hair, tattoos and body piercing, that anyone taking on these affectations has to survive a mighty battle with the world, which sees them as losers and will inevitably treat them as such. I guess I always had a reluctant admiration for his guts.

Chapter Eight

One must wait until evening to see how splendid the day has been.

When we first got quite crazy about Ravello, we were staying in the Hotel Parsifal. It had been a convent, but for some reason or other it had failed and the nuns sold up to an hotelier. A quiet, peaceful place at the northern end of the town on the Via D'Anna. The owner told us about Gore Vidal, the famous American writer, who lived in Ravello. Apparently, he had visited the town when he was in the US Army in World War 2 and had always wanted to live there. Eventually, in 1972, he was able to buy the villa La Rondinaia (The Swallow's Nest). It was built by Lord Grimthorpe, the owner of the Villa Cimbrone, for his daughter in 1930. The story of Grimthorpe and the Cimbrone gardens is written elsewhere, and so is the story of the Rondinaia. Sue and I became spellbound by Gore Vidal and consequently we read some of his books and were able to visit his house after it was sold in 2004.

Gore is famous for his witty sayings. However, most of them require an insider's knowledge of the American political scene in order to get the joke. He said once that a particular senator had 'All the qualities of a dog, except the loyalty' and 'Whenever a friend succeeds, a little something in me dies.' Not exactly Ken Dodd, but funny in a slightly objectionable sort of way.

I want to meander in my mind about Italy, but this talk of writers has reminded me that I saw in the paper this morning that a Mr William May of Godalming in Surrey was run over by an oil tanker and killed outright last week. He was 34 years old. Well, he was a writer of a kind whom I remember well. All teachers have these sorts of memories which are hard to erase. He was fourteen years old when I taught him in my English class. He was not the ripest tomato in the vacuum pack, and as it happens both his parents were also killed in a road accident. So Billy May was brought up by his grandparents. I felt sure I had kept a piece of his writing from twenty years ago, just before I retired. I had a look in some of my old files and eventually brought it out. Normally he never rose above a D for any English work, but I see that I gave him a B+ for content in this case but an E for punctuation.

A Story About old People
by Billy May

Old people are usually nice but some are mean and deaf and you have to shout for them to hear you and they drink coffee all the time and read and fall to sleep and you have to wake them up and they get a lot of attention and they almost live in the hospital and they have big glasses and no hair and they have hearing aids and they have to be helped to eat their food and they eat it with no manners and they take loads of pills to help them go to sleep but I don't know why when they fall to sleep anyway and they have fake teeth and they have to stick their fake teeth to their gums and they tell you off a lot when you are not doing anything their favourite thing is to read the newspapers and they drive smart cars and young people drive old cars and once you're over 60 that means you're old and they buy loads of stuff for christmas and they sit at home a lot and do nothing and they think wow this is exciting and they say I am tired and go to bed.

In a way, I am glad that Billy never got to grow old. He clearly didn't look forward to it.

Teaching is not a bad job. It has its moments. But try admitting that you are a teacher while at a dinner party or any social occasion and you immediately have to contend with. 'What do you do with all those holidays?' or 'Could you tutor my daughter to get through the eleven plus?' or in one case, 'Have you ever been mugged in class?'

Admitting that you teach in a state comprehensive school is the equivalent of saying you have given up real life to work in some god forsaken ghetto where no civilized person would be seen dead.

I tried teaching in a Primary school for a year and this was even worse. Being a man amongst all those little children and female teachers was hard enough on the nerves. I began by liking the kids quite a lot, but their illogical and inconsequential answers to many of my questions eventually got me down. They also insisted on calling me Miss.

'Miss, Miss, Miss' I recall one ten year old kept calling, jumping up in her seat and flinging one arm in the air like a mad member of the Waffen-SS in a Hitler parade. 'Sit down Alison, keep quiet, put your hand down,' I kept shouting, and getting angrier and angrier. 'But Miss, you're bleeding!' she finally gasped. And indeed, I had cut myself shaving and there was blood all down the side of my face.

Another time I spent ten minutes explaining the topic of sound, using rice in a plastic cup; something I had prepared the night before and was quite proud of.

'Any questions?' I asked, and a seven year old put his hand up immediately and said 'My Daddy's got a jacket just like yours Miss,'

Eventually, I had to give up and get back to secondary school work where, although the kids could be difficult and even surly at times, it was a semi-adult and more male environment, and I did not receive unsubtle insinuations of paedophilia when talking to local worthies in the pub.

It is the media that twists the public mind about schools as well as teaching in general. Every reference to educational institutions in the newspapers is about failure or lower standards. Quite unjustified, as teachers have more investment in success than most working folk. Our jobs depend on it. I once had to drive around the north circular in London at four o'clock when children were coming out of two or three hundred schools. I noticed that there were thousands of them, all well-behaved and even boringly so, walking home with their books under their arms. Whereas according to most news items, kids were supposed to be running feral in the city.

Every TV play that contains a scene in a primary school seems to dress the children in blazers and little peaked caps like the prep schools of the 1930s. Writers and reporters have been stuck in the days of Billy Bunter for the past fifty years.

I was talking about Ravello again, and wandered off the point.

We wanted to retire there from the first day that we visited the place. We saw a chef up a fig tree gathering fruit and Sue and I both had the same instant thought,
        'This is the place!'
A few days later a local resident asked if he could buy my trousers; they had the latest fashionable zipped pockets all over them. Naturally I refused, but it confirmed our view that this was our sort of town.
The fact that DH Lawrence, Virginia Woolf, Graham Greene and Thomas Mann had stayed there and written about it, was enough to clinch it. Something of all these writers might rub off on us. As a matter of fact I did write a couple of stories about Ravello, as I found the atmosphere truly inspiring. The experience of our favourite hotel started me off with this one.

Italian Holiday Payback

When Signor Alberto Giordano saw the plump old German tourist enter the lobby, he knew that he had seen him before, a long time ago. A padrone remembers these things. A few metres off the piazza, in sight of the old duomo, the modest family hotel of Villa Cristina has welcomed guests for fifty years, some of them the same ones for the same number of years. But this one had never been a guest, he was certain of that. Alberto prided himself, he never forgot a face.

The main square, the piazza, of Ravello has seen remarkable sights; from Hollywood movie stars to jazz concerts, from Arab architects to American tourists.

Through peace and war people of all nations have made the 300 metre climb up from Amalfi. They always stayed for an hour or two of heaven in this little retreat. Now, in the 21st century, it boasts a dozen top hotels and twice that many world class restaurants; yet the streets are still too narrow for cars. If you want a cheap package don't try Ravello, but if it is charm, quiet and a little expensive luxury, then you might find it there.

Alberto checked the bookings and saw the man's name was Dr Heinrich Von Nadel. Well, every other German was a Herr Doktor of something or other, and 'Von' was far too pretentious for these days. He looked up from the keyboard and found the man had disappeared down the hallway to his room, his grey wife in tow.

Later, in bed, he told Rosaria that he had seen a face he ought to remember.

'Go so sleep caro,' she murmured as she turned away, 'We have the Rozzi wedding tomorrow.'

At breakfast by the pool the padrone watched Von Nadel. He was fat, sleek and his wife looked disgruntled and frightened, a bad combination in his experience. Alberto began to use his brain. The German must be at least 85, probably more. That made him old enough to have been in the war. Alberto's generation never had to explain which war; there was only one and Germany had lost it. The Giordano family had been in the hotel business during that time when he and his older brother Donato were only kids. Many Nazi officers had been based in Ravello. It was taken over by order of Field Marshall

Kesselring as a rest and recreation centre for his crack Panzer troops. They knew that the allied invasion was coming and the partying was tremendous. Alberto and Donato used to help as waiters, and were popular with most of the German officers. Some, however, treated the youngsters like slaves. There was one in particular who drank more than the rest, Alberto never knew his name, but searching in his memory he wondered...

Donato ran his own restaurant in the Via Roma. It was famous the world over for its local cuisine. It was one of those family places where there was no written menu; it was all in the head of Donato. He was the family genius when it came to cooking, Alberto's skills lay in administration. Each brother had fulfilled his own boyhood dream. It was Donato who could not walk properly however, he had been shot in the foot and in the chest by a drunken Panzer officer. Alberto determined to get his brother up to the Villa Cristina to observe this Von Nadel character. He was becoming more and more certain where and when he had seen him.

It was September 1943 and they all heard the big naval guns off Salerno. The officers were getting particularly drunk. They knew that many of them would not see out the month. Alberto remembered being so terrified that he wanted to run down into the wine cellar with Mama. He could not bring himself to serve at table, he was only nine years old. Donato, who was fourteen, seemed like a man to him then; he told Alberto that he wanted to be part of the war. The Germans were supposed to be on the Italian's side, but they despised Italy he knew. Secretly, like their parents, both boys hoped the Americans would win. Unfortunately,

Donato repeated this aspiration within hearing of the officer who was so often drunk. That evening the man was incoherent with fear, rage and limoncello. He pulled out his revolver and took a potshot at Donato. All the other Germans tried to pull him back. Then they claimed he was only joking and had intended to miss. One bullet through the foot and one lodged in the lung, Donato was driven to their own small clinic by two worried officers and his life hung in the balance for three days. When he came back a month after surgery, the Germans had gone. The allied invasion had swept everyone north to defend Rome. Young Donato was cured of his desire to become part of the war. He had discovered exactly what it could be like.

Alberto finished his chores in the small office at the rear of the Villa Cristina and strolled down into the piazza and along the narrow Via Roma to drink their usual morning coffee with his brother. The two of them were still very close. They were partners in both the restaurant and the hotel, although each ran his own establishment. The restaurant, Donatello's, was open but empty at this time of day. His brother specialised in evening meals and it hardly came alive until seven pm. Alberto sat and they both drank their espresso silently for five minutes. Donato hardly woke up until midday and Alberto knew better than to try and tax his brain at 11 o'clock. Finally, he could wait no longer.

'Can you come over to the hotel later today? There is someone I would like you to see.'

'Sounds very mysterious.' Donato coughed as he put down his cup and lit another cigarette. His lung was bad enough without the smoking, but he would not be told.

'Someone from the old days has come to stay, that's all I will say at the moment, but I think you will be very interested.' Alberto then had to hurry back to assist with the preparations for the Rozzi wedding.

It was three o'clock before Donato arrived at the Villa Cristina and looked for his brother. There were no guests around and most of the staff were fully engaged with the wedding reception in the garden at the rear. Alberto appeared and he was in a hurry.

'Can you leave your work tonight and come to dinner here?' he said breathlessly.

"I suppose so, but why is it so important? Surely you can tell me?'

'The person I want you to meet will be here this evening. He has gone out now. I am sure you will want to meet him.'

Donato agreed, and looking very puzzled, went back to his restaurant to tell the assistant chef that he would be in charge that night.

The street lamps around the piazza shone their yellow orbs making ochre pools on the stone paving. Donato walked sedately across the well-lit square in his new white jacket. He felt at peace with the world and looking forward to meeting this old acquaintance that Alberto had evidently scraped up for him from somewhere. Young parents stood around talking animatedly and small children ran in and around them laughing. Everyone was in their best clothes for the Passaggiata, the Italian evening stroll.

Alberto greeted his smiling brother at the lobby and gestured for him to follow down the steps to the dining room. He walked across the room to where the fat German and his pale wife were sitting at their table with a bottle of wine. They were silent and unaware of the approach of the brothers.

Alberto stopped by the table and spoke rather stiffly.

'Signor Von Nadel, allow me to introduce to you my brother Donato Giordano.'

He watched as Donato stepped forward and made a little bow,

'Buona sera Signor,' he said. Von Nadel stood up with some difficulty and extended his hand rather formally towards his companion.

'This is my wife Helmund'

Alberto heard his brother cry out, 'Do you not recognise me then?' The woman looked surprised to be addressed so forcibly and then she smiled, 'Donato? Klein Donato!'

Donato turned back to Alberto and slapped him on the back,

'What a surprise! You remember when I got shot in the chest all those years ago?'

'Of course.'

'This is doctor Von Nadel, he saved my life! Helmund was his nurse then.' He rushed over to fling his arms around the embarrassed wife, 'So you two married after all?'He turned to Von Nadel,

'I can never thank you enough doctor.'

Alberto stepped back from the table and cleared his throat.

'I knew you would be pleased,' he said, and he turned to the old doctor who was now grinning with pleasure.

'Of course there will be no charge for this hotel. Please stay as long as you like.'

Chapter Nine

The older we get, the fewer things seem worth waiting in line for.

I sometimes wonder if our sense of time is controlled by the frequency of our heart beats. When we are little children our hearts beat much faster. According to Wikipedia a three-year-old's heart races away at 217 beats per minute, I could get a lot done with all those spasms adding up. So when I was very young, the time seemed to pass very slowly. I was packing a lot of heart beats into a minute, and an hour seemed to take up a lot of my life. Well it did, it was using up 13,020 pumps of my existence in one hour. But by 85 years of age the old ticker has slowed down to around 135 pulses every sixty seconds. Nowadays, I only get 8,100 beats to an hour, which is almost half as many as in those childhood days. So time seems to pass much more quickly. An hour is soon gone. Small birds are the same. Their hearts flutter and race when you pick them up and to them of course, a couple of years is a lifetime.

I was thinking of this when I invited my old friend Dave Bucknell to Sunday lunch this week. I spoke to him on Thursday, and when he turned up on the family doorstep at noon on Sunday I was ashamed to say that I had forgotten that I had asked him. The time had flown so quickly because I remembered only that I was *going* to invite him, not that I already had. After a few laughs about it and the sucking down of a couple of gin and tonics, Dave in his good humoured way forgave me and we settled down to roast shoulder of lamb, and Yorkshire pud etc. Dave seemed a bit puzzled by Sue and I commenting together aloud that, 'There is nothing like a good leg of lamb.'

'But thith ith a thoulder of lamb,' he protested.

'It's a family joke,' we told him.

'But what ith the joke?'

Sue and I looked at one another and had to admit that weren't sure, but that we always said this when we had lamb.

'Tho, if you have a leg of lamb, you always say that there ith nothing like a thoulder?'

'Exactly' I assured him. 'We think it's hilarious.'

Poor Dave just shook his head wildly with disbelief and showered even more dandruff onto his roast lunch. He soon consoled himself with several gulps of my favourite Chilean Cabernet Sauvignon. Then remarked on the fact that I was drinking water with my own meal.

'I thought you had given up that thtuff. Have you theen what it doeth to the bottom of boatth?'

'I am just cutting down on the old wine intake this week. The doc told me that he had found some blood in my alcohol stream.' I replied in an attempt to lighten the mood.' But once Dave had got onto his high horse there was no stopping him.

'Everybody'th mad on water thethe days. The bottleth of it cotht more than petrol. The young go around like infanth all day long thwigging water out of feeding bottleth. They even have containerth with teatth of thome thort. Clearly they have all regrethed to thuch an exthtent that I darethay you will thoon have to be twenty-five before you can be potty trained.'

We all laughed at that, but there was a serious thought in his rhetoric which did not go unacknowledged. There is a lot of water drunk by youngsters in a way that we never felt necessary years ago. If we ever had to quench our thirst out of the tap we used to add a spoonful of Andrews Liver salts to spice it up a bit!

My thoughts turned to Beowulf when Dave spoke of infants because I have always thought that my eldest was exhibiting a sort of Peter Pan syndrome. The thing is, he is not alone. So many 30 to 50 year old men these days have never really grown up. They have dropped out of anything that requires responsibility. They are obsessed with celebrity. Grown men watch 'Strictly Come Dancing' on the TV. Something as astonishingly lightweight as football takes over their lives. It's no wonder that so many women are turning to one another for companionship. If I was a woman, I would definitely be as gay as a cricket.

I steered Dave to the sitting room to give Sue a chance to re-fill the jar marked 'Strong Italian Coffee' with our usual decaffeinated brand. Neither of us can take real coffee and it is a harmless deception that always fools our guests but does no damage. Unfortunately, ten minutes later Dave said, 'Thith coffee tathe like decaff, are you thure it'th real?' So the game was up. I promised him a double shot of brandy in every cup from now on, to preserve his silence, and he jumped like a kangaroo at the prospect. When he left he thanked both of us for a good lunch and a laugh. I am not sure how happy he is living alone.

Sue and I got talking about happiness in bed last night. Happiness is a strange concept. We all claim to feel it from time to time, but it seems to mean different things to each one of us. All sorts of people have tried to define it, and where does it end? Do we even know when we are happy? I know I am happy in bed with Sue.

We usually know when we are unhappy. Some people would claim to be unhappy all the time; my son Beowulf says he is. Maybe those people are depressed, but we have seen depressed people become quite happy, even if only for a few minutes. It is a complicated business.

It is certainly difficult to tell if another creature is happy. I can listen to Korky purring and by a slight anthropomorphic inference say that she is happy. But we have no real way of knowing. In just the same way, we may look across a room at a young married couple laughing in the first throes of marriage and say 'Look how happy they are.' Humans are complex creatures, and the assumption that two people chuckling together means happiness is, well, laughable. They each might be flirting with the notion of murdering the other.

We both started to wonder if happiness depends to a certain extent upon intelligence? This is not referring to high intelligence but to a degree of awareness higher than say, a snail or an insect? We regularly impute happiness to our pets, to animals kept in zoos and to certain of our own unfortunate fellow human beings who, having limited abilities, are unable to look after themselves. It is usual to reassure ourselves by saying, 'Well she is very happy where she is.' It is important to our own sense of what is fitting, that those for whom we are in some sense responsible, are happy. Parents checking on their children in school, often say that they don't mind too much about their academic progress 'As long as they are happy.' They may not always mean it, but they want the world to believe it. It is deemed anti-social in our western culture, to place almost anything else, except perhaps health, above happiness.

Sue asked me seriously if I knew when happiness begins? Would our newborn grandson be happy at this moment? Obviously, if he were born in a ditch and abandoned by a fleeing mother, out of her head on some illegal substance, the chances are that the screaming infant will feel a little let down. But, as a rule, all the baby requires is food, warmth and security. These provide life and contentment. It is doubtful whether 'happiness', however it may be characterised, is within the consciousness of such a young being. As the child matures over days and weeks and begins to associate its mother with the provision of these goodies, a relationship with another person will develop. Signs of pleasure are evident when baby senses mother approaching and feeding. It rather looks as if pleasure, at least, is to be associated at an early stage in a person's life, with the love of another. Of course, pleasure should not be confused with happiness. Such confusion is what has lead to the pursuit of pleasure, and to the consequent destruction of happiness as a result, in many peoples' lives.

Still, the idea of happiness, and its existence as a goal, must start somewhere. Children are often said to be 'happy' and are frequently asked if they are happy and will reply dutifully 'Yes'. This may not mean that they are, but merely that they have learned that it is the required answer. In the same way a child may be asked the more open-ended question 'How are you feeling now?' and may reply 'I am happy.' The reasons for such a reply may be many, even with a quite young person. They may mean 'Go away I am busy playing.' or it may just be a reflex response like saying 'Bye bye' and waving a tiny hand when leaving their house.

It is even possible for youngsters to be made so miserable so often, that they have never known what it is to be happy. When we consider the cases of two year olds who have been beaten, starved, stood in boiling water and burnt with cigarettes, it is easy to conclude that they will never have learnt what it is to be happy. Such victims may well grow to believe the evil above all evils, that to be in severe pain and hated is what 'happiness' means.

So it is at least arguable that happiness has to be learned, and that we may not begin our lives with the idea of happiness already established in our minds. Clearly the lesser experiences of pleasure and pain are with us from the start. They are evidently present in quite simple animals. It has even been argued that these sensations are present in plants. But happiness is different. It is conceivable for humans to be happy while in severe pain, and also to be happy without necessarily seeking pleasurable activities. Of course, it is possible to take pleasure both by inflicting and receiving pain. However, it is doubtful whether what most people would call true happiness results from either of those experiences. Nevertheless, it is something to reflect on, and such considerations even help to further our notions of what defines both happiness and pleasure and where they differ from one another. Many people describe their own states of happiness in ways which show that they nearly always occur unexpectedly. I may be weeding the garden or cooking, and find myself humming a tune. Then gradually it occurs to me that I am feeling happy.

Conversely, people have also reported how they have set out deliberately to cheer themselves up, to try and be a little bit happier and it has failed. A conscious effort to be happy is not always successful. People sometimes say that they remember an occasion in the past, and, looking back, they realise how happy they were then; although perhaps they did not take it in at the time.

Chapter Ten

Being young is beautiful, but being old is comfortable.

Now the baby has arrived! Either it is amazingly early or we were completely misinformed about the date of conception. Anyway, it is a boy weighing seven pounds, which in my experience is pretty healthy. We now have a wonderful grandson who is in no way, even accidentally, related to us. Does anybody mind? Not at all. This tiny creature is already loved by the whole family. Even Beowulf was caught going 'Who's a lovely boy then?' bent over the carry cot; (or Eco Rocking Moses basket that Jenny calls it.) We are all happy at the moment. In keeping with our family tradition of embarrassing a small child with its name, the baby has been called Ahab. The first name is not so much a problem as its surname. Which mother will it be named after? Huntingdon or Jenny's surname Bigelow? They are considering a double barrelled solution; think about it?

While we were all thinking about this challenge. I got another of those phone calls just when I was enjoying the TV news from Russia Today.

'Is that Mr Huntingdon? How are you today?'

It was the cheery woman with the Mumbai accent yet again. Instead of slamming the phone down in an attempt to deafen the caller, I decided to answer,

'Well I am suffering somewhat because of my irritable bowel syndrome; also my old wound is throbbing but I don't like to talk about it. The arthritis is keeping my mind off the toothache, but but basically speaking, since the open heart surgery I have not been able to perform my husbandly functions if you know what I mean...' There was a couple of seconds pause and the lady asked, "Are you interested in double glazing at all?"

I put down the phone very gently and smiled with an inner peace which had not visited me since landing back at base in the early morning in a totally unscathed Lancaster in 1944.

I wonder who the other people are that get these cold calls? Obviously people with telephones. At one time that would have been limited to the middle and upper classes. Nowadays, even those of us who have filled in the telephone preference forms, still get the calls.

Mind you, Sue says that the class hierarchies in England are still as complicated as any Indian caste system, and I agree. Admittedly they are subtle, which is why they are so interesting. It is just that most people are unwilling to admit their existence. If you are one of the top dogs today, is it fashionable to deny that there are any social differences in the UK.

'Jack's as good as his master' is whispered cynically in private clubs and behind the most expensive front doors across the land. The very phrase gives away the attitudes of the speaker in one short sentence. He in no way believes himself to be 'Jack'. In more public places the lips are pursed forwards, shoulders shrugged and 'It's a bloody a democracy now,' is the cry.

If you are unfortunate enough to slot into a less privileged stratum, you will hear almost the same sentiments expressed; but they are muttered in a futile hope that it might be true, never with any conviction. 'Well, we're all the same now aren't we?' or 'Who do *they* think they are?' The social panic, which grips all levels of our society, is the terror of being accused of snobbery, whether inverted or convoluted. It is this intense fear of admitting anything openly, which inhibits the discussion of social status in England; Scotland and Wales of course, may well be different.

In England there will always be some reason that can be found for looking down on another person.

'She was wearing a nylon overall' one woman will say of another, and that is enough to elicit encouraging nods of mutual superiority from her audience. A man is unlikely to comment aloud on another man's appearance, but he will note privately and silently that the dreadful fellow was wearing white socks, or a blazer with a badge on the pocket, and that will be remembered and counted against him for ever.

If you think that this does not still go on, then try to visit planet earth sometime!

Last night Sue said she wanted to give me a treat. She made sure we had a scrappy lunch, a half a tomato each with some strange leaves from Waitrose, accompanied by a tiny bit of corned beef. I love corned beef. It was a cheap delicacy just after the war and rather looked down upon by the chattering classes.

Anyway the treat in the evening was to be a ready-meal chilli-con-carne. It came in a synthetic bowl which had been sealed by a transparent plastic sheet on the top. But could we open it? Sue tried with her fingers and nearly tore her nail off. I attempted with a pair of scissors which made no impression at all. I realise now that a great punishment for pensioners would be a prison where everybody had to get at their meals which would be sealed into plastic covered containers. Finally Sue stabbed the container with the bread knife and emptied it into a saucepan rice and chilli together. When we thought it was ready Sue doled it out onto our plates, and I opened a bottle of Australian Cabernet . The chilli tasted burnt and the rice was like little pellets of gravel, quite inedible. I looked at the packet to see if Sue had got the timing wrong and read

'*Place unopened pack into the microwave or oven.* We don't have a microwave, and I could not believe that plastic would not burn in the oven. But there it was in white on red. '*Place unopened.*' I suppose the heat would have dissolved the glue under the cover. Well, that was our evening ruined. I had to get in the Jag and drive down to the chippy for two cod and wedges. I suppose Beowulf would have used one of his dreadful modern expressions like, 'At the end of the day' 'It all went pear-shaped' 'Know what I mean?'

Quite without warning, the next morning, a young man of about twenty-two knocked on our front door. Why he didn't press the perfectly good bell I have recently installed is beyond me. Anyhow, he said that my son Beowulf had sent him to check up on the special plants he had growing in our garden and to harvest a few if it was all right with us. He actually had a crumpled bit of paper signed by Beo to say that he was authorised. Obviously, Sue shouted that he was welcome and would he like a cup of tea? He said that he preferred coffee if that was OK (Excuse *him*). The lad then introduced himself as Alex.

He shambled in and I noticed that his jeans belt had evidently broken and they were hanging halfway down his behind, showing a sizeable section of grubby underpants. He was also carrying a half-litre bottle of water with a kind of teat arrangement from which he took a swig every three or four minutes. I felt it was only kind to mention his belt problem and he thanked me very politely but took no notice. After tea he went into the garden and filled a small brown paper bag with the tops of about half of Beo's plants, which have grown considerably in the last four months. I asked Alex what they were and he said, 'Just weed'. I thought they looked a bit like some sort of Chinese decorative bush, but there you go. No accounting for taste. He thanked us for the tea and on his way out pressed twenty pounds in tenners into my hand. I was flabbergasted, but he pushed off very happy and waved to us both as he went out of the front gate. Later, I phoned Beowulf and asked about Alex, was he kosher and all that sort of thing. He assured me that everything was hunky dory and not to worry. When I mentioned the money, he went ballistic.

'The cheeky bastard!' he said, 'he should have given you fifty at least.'

'Whatever for?' I said. Beo then went very quiet.

'Don't you know?' he asked quietly.

'Not a clue,' I had to say, being honest.

'Good on you Dad, keep it that way, know what I mean?' he said, laughed and put down the phone.

I truly suspect now that those weeds may be some sort of drug, you never know these days. I may be old but I am not stupid.

It is time we had another conference and looked at our finances. Sue and I decided to have it in bed, where we look at one another, and neither of us is behind a door or has wandered into another room. So, when we had settled in, I had drunk my cocoa and Sue had finished her exercises (For her knees and ankles, well, one knee and one ankle really; the doctor examined her ankle and told her it was shaky due to her age. Sue quite sharply responded that her other ankle was exactly the same age). This put the cat among the pigeons, I can tell you. Doctors are losing their social status enough already without old ladies taking the Mick as well!

Anyway, as were talking about the money from my book, most unexpected and welcome, I suddenly remembered that in 1945 I had come home and given my mother £100 which was part of my RAF gratuity. She had put it into a Post Office savings book in my name and then paid about £2 a month into it for me until the day she died. That was in 1972. I asked Sue if she knew where it was. She said she had no idea, but it would most likely be in the attic with my old uniform and cap in a cardboard box. I got out of bed immediately and went upstairs and pulled down the loft ladder. It was hard on my bare feet but nothing ventured etc. I climbed up and found the box, covered in dust and lo and behold! There was the PO savings book dated October 1945, the month I was demobbed. I brought it down to the bedroom and we both opened it together and looked inside. There were the figures, an initial deposit of £100 and 324 additional entries of £2 each until 1972. a total of £748. Sue got very excited, because unlike me, she is numerate and understands compound interest. I was happy to have the £748 but she reckoned it would be more than that after all these years. We decided to take it to the post Office in the morning and see what they had to say.

They had to send the book away, but eventually it came back updated to 2012 and the savings came to £5,253.01. It began to look as if we might get our dream villa in Italy after all. At least we could afford the patio!

Chapter Eleven

The quickest way to double your money is to fold it and put it back into your pocket.

Another envelope arrived a few days later from the publisher. I asked Sue to open it as I couldn't bear the suspense. Her face was a picture when she handed it over.

This time it contained a cheque for £2,030. The accompanying letter explained that a couple of American universities had bought copies as textbooks for their history of art students, and that Amazon had agreed to advertise the title. A new cover had been designed by the publisher's own in-house artist. It was selling well in Canada and Australia, and it would be on show at the next Frankfurt Book Fair.

This took Sue and me onto cloud nine. I warned her not to say a word either to Beo or Scarlett or to the neighbours.

I trotted into the sitting room and was relaxing in a happy daydream of facing up to the Italian planning authorities, while watching our favourite video of 'Three Coins in The Fountain'. Mentally, I had designed a cool marble hall, and a Palladian entrance to our ideal retirement home. The phone rang and on lifting the receiver, I heard the voice saying,

'My name is Ricky, how are you today? I am calling from Andover double glazing...' Before he could go any further I had shouted, 'Get stuffed you useless bastard!' and banged the receiver down with a most satisfactory thump.

I sat back with a very contented smile. At last things were going our way.

About a minute later the phone rang again. I ignored it and let Sue answer. She came into the sitting room and told me that the man she had booked last week to put in our new kitchen window, had just called, and what on earth had I said to him?

I crept quietly outside and drove down to the club. There was no-one in the bar except Jacky my dream barmaid and so I asked her to join me for a snifter. I had a double Famous Grouse and she had a half of lager. She was too experienced a girl to ask for a fancy drink.

'Had a bit of luck on the horses then?' she asked, and leaned forward on the bar top exposing half a kilo of freckled yet tempting bosom framed in white lace. I think the commodore had briefed her on the correct protocol for barmaids in any decent yacht club.

'No, just a small royalty from my publisher,' I said in my best mock modesty voice. I told her about my *faux pas* with the telephone and she really saw the funny side of the story. Either that or she was panting for another half. Any way, I bought her a second one in gratitude for lifting my soul.

After half an hour of outrageous flirting on my part, and some good-natured and innocent kindness towards an old man on Jacky's, Dave Bucknell arrived with the news that he had been invited to the Buckingham Palace garden party in June.

'What am I going to wear old thon?' he asked, as I handed him his usual gin and tonic.

'You sound like my missus on a good day,' I said, 'Bottoms up.'

'Yeth I know but it'th true. I can't turn up at the Palathe gateth in my betht thuit. I've had it for hundredth of yearth. It wath made for me in Hong Kong in the nineteen fiftieth by Thin Jelly Belly in Nathan Road. I wore it on leave after 'Thueth.'

'You will have to get a new one, no question,' I said.

'The invite says blazerth may be worn.'

'Well there you are then, you've got that blazer you wear for the yacht club lunches.'

'It'th jutht as old as the thuit. I had it knocked up at the thame time ath the suit; and you thpilt tomato thauce down it last time if you recall.'

'I thought we cleaned that off with turps?' I asked.

'Exactly, now it thmells like an art thudent's armpit.'

'Then you'll have to go to Oxfam and find another blazer; god knows there are plenty of posh blokes around here whose wives give away their old duds at the drop of a Burberry.'

'You don't often have a good idea old man, but that ith a corker. I'll do it tomorrow, cheerth'

By the next day the window installer had finished and gone home. I never saw him again and Sue said she had given him a big tip which made him crack a grin.

Anyhow, Scarlett and Jenny arrived just after lunch with our new grandson Ahab. He is a charmer, long eyelashes and plenty of dark hair. I think his donor must have been a film star! The two mothers wanted to go shopping in town and so left baby with Sue and me for the first time. They also left some modern gunge in a jar to feed him with if he cried. He actually screamed like a vulture as soon as they were out of the door. Sue looked a trifle anxious at this point saying she was a bit out of practice. Foolish me, I volunteered to do the honours and got out our old baby chair from the garage.

No Gemini space rendezvous is more tricky than connecting a spoonful of homogenized bleeagh with the eight -month old mouth. The small spoon is dipped into the stamped carrot or prunes, barley and bacon or whatever, and launched
like a brown streak towards the semi-toothed target. It is just at this moment that a passing fly, or bee, catches the attention of the little infant. As I mentally fired the retro-rockets, the tiny head turned 180 degrees to right and left and the minced liver and rice became a Salvador Dali moustache stretching from ear to ear. Try again. Ahab is crying out with hunger and frustration now, blaming me for mismanaging the feeding operation.
In-flight refuelling this time. I am Walter Mitty at the controls.
I fill the old spoon and gingerly ease the control column forward, gently now, gently, the little inlet orifice looms tantalizingly ahead, dribbling slightly, with a rabbit nudge of white tooth showing. Over the plastic tray, spoon with load still intact, over the edge of the bib now and still coming. What has happened to the target? The mouth! It's not there! Suddenly the

whole head isn't there. He has ducked under the incoming spoon flat on to the plastic tray and is peering downwards like a commando over a cliff. That's it, of course, he had forgotten to check if his feet were still attached to his body. Sitting up equally suddenly, the back of his head catches the underside of the spoon which I am still holding like a tiny fencing foil in front of me. With the tray and hair full of gravy and, as yet, not a single vitamin past the baby lips, I stubbornly dig into the plate of bleeagh! which I am holding in my left hand, and come up with eek! a finger! Oh no! The 58th variety. Especially tinned for modern cannibals. It isn't, it belongs of course to the hand of my grandson, now satisfied about his toes but extremely unsatisfied dinner-wise. He has stuffed about four pounds of cotton bib down his throat with the other hand, and more is still being poured down in wads.

I put down the spoon and as carefully as a butcher drawing a

chicken, extract a yard of saliva-sodden bunny rabbits from his

mouth. The next load goes straight in without effort, it is as if a vacuum cleaner nozzle had plucked it from the spoon. One draw-back however, he has clenched his brand new teeth on the spoon and try as I might I cannot get it back. I pull, wriggle; a mad Alsatian gripping the last bone on earth would be easier to deal with.

The only solution is to find another spoon. The useless patent

feeding one will have to do. But now my grandchild is jumping up and down like a football supporter and waving both arms in a kind of frenetic butterfly backstroke, harness jingling and the spoon like a bit between his teeth. The room suddenly becomes as noisy and as entertaining as Billy Smart's ring.

He calms down as unexpectedly as he began and immediately starts to trace complicated and artistic abstracts with his fingers in the spilt mess on the tray.

He refuses to look up.

I make clucking noises chu chu, chu chu

I make boo noises boo boo boo,

Fatal mistake, I say patacake, patacake baker's man and he re-

sponds at once, spattering little flips of homogenized stuff across my trousers.

My daughter comes back in earlier than I had expected.

      'Haven't you fed him yet? 'she says, 'Men are useless!'

She grabs the spoon from his mouth, the plate from my limp

hands, and has given him the lot before I can creep out of the room.

Some time ago Sue and I joined the University of the Third Age or U3A as it is known. Sue had this continuing thirst for knowledge while I had a consuming thirst for wine. As there was an Italian language group and three wine-tasting sections we were both quite happy. The Italian group ended up being held in the house of a local worthy who had political aspirations. These consisted of an overwhelming admiration for Attila the Hun and a desire to return all immigrants since 1066 to their foreign homelands. I was happy to duck out of this commitment as I find that having vaguely left-wing views in our town is like being part of a secret underground. You have to wait for signs from your acquaintances, rather like the Freemasons, to tell whether it is OK to express some mild views on town planning or the NHS. When the vicar's wife announces that all drug dealers should be shot or that the working class children don't deserve to go to good schools, it is best to keep silent and try to watch the reactions of others. Should you protest, then it's no more cucumber sandwiches for you.

So I volunteered for the wine tasting. The wine appreciation group met in the members' houses once a fortnight and it came to be my main source of social contact, apart from the yacht club of course. When Sue used to make all our arrangements we were always lunching with other couples or having people over to coffee, but now all that had faded away. The wine group, however, was lively and although most were elderly women, by the end of the tasting afternoons, tongues wagged freely and sometimes I told a slightly risqué joke, if I could summon one up from my tricky memory. I had always enjoyed wine; my special favourites were any full-bodied French reds. This group had broadened my appreciation and I had even found a couple of white wines that I liked, a white Rioja and a fruity New Zealand Sauvignon Blanc.

One particular afternoon I recall, we were meeting in the well-kept flat of Mrs Marjorie Burton, the grey charmless widow of Captain Burton RN. As the hostess, it was her choice of wines. There were two acidic Eastern European rosés and two whites, a

Chardonnay and some ghastly Italian stuff that I had to spit out at once into the plastic bucket provided. This was unusual as most members swallowed their third of a glass and came back for more, but I had become rather fussy and felt I had to draw the line somewhere. Dennis Smart, a garrulous retired salesman across the room, winked and gestured a thumb up at me pretending to admire my honesty. Another widow, Barbara Garrard, sitting to the right of Dennis polished off her cheap Italian Pinot Grigio, and raised her empty glass to me. Big violet hair, plenty of bosom and large false eyelashes opened and then lowered, as if to say look what you are missing...

My God! I am Mr Popular today, I thought to myself. I smiled weakly at the others and took a dry organic biscuit from the little Chinese basket provided by our well-travelled hostess.

The meeting broke up and the elderly group moved slowly outside to their cars. Barbara Garrard spoke softly into my ear as she went past.

    'See you in two weeks then.'

    'What? Oh yes, two weeks time Mrs Garrard.'

    'Barbara please.'

I took the Jag through the big wrought-iron gates of the apartment block and sped home. I really needed that single malt waiting in the kitchen cabinet.

That evening I opened a fresh bottle of Barossa Valley Shiraz and drank the whole £8.50 with our heated up TV dinner from Tesco's that was our Wednesday special.

I cut down on the whisky but increased the red wine. During the next fortnight I went through three bottles of Bodegas Montecillo Gran Reserva Rioja, two of South Australian Cab Sav, three bottles of a new Argentinian very smooth Merlot that I had found in my local wine store, and one bottle of the New Zealand Sauvignon Blanc that Dave Bucknell had recommended a month ago. I went to the Plough and Horseman twice for lunch during that time and drank a couple of glasses of whatever the house red was. Altogether an enjoyable couple of weeks for an elderly retired Comprehensive School teacher. My face began to take on a slightly redder hue and my distinguished-looking white hair fell in two elegant quiffs over each ear. Without Sue to put the brakes on, I would have become even more reckless.

The time came for the next wine group and I decided to walk as the host this time was a near neighbour called Tom Best. No need to risk the Jaguar, I could sample all the wines I wanted and no driving problem. Tom stood at his front door to greet the little party. As I entered the living room, Barbara Garrard beckoned me across the floor. her even larger black lashes fluttered and an even lower neckline wobbled. She leaned forward and smiled like a toothpaste advert.

'Peter, come and sit by me on the sofa I've saved you a place.' I sat down and felt the merry widow patting my knee. Tom produced six bottles that he had selected from an exclusive local vintner. He had printed out all their details and prices on a couple of sheets of A4 to hand round.

Barbara took the first sample and looking into my eyes said,

'Bottoms up then.'

'What? Oh yes, well cheers,' and we clinked glasses. I thought the 2005 Fleury tasted slightly like a farmyard, but pleasantly drinkable with a slight appley tinge. Certainly superior to anything we had tried in the last couple of months.

'I believe I have something even better than this at home,' remarked Barbara looking at me from under those lashes again. I wondered whether she had her own cellar. I thought it tactful not to ask, in case she lived in a flat.

'Have a nibble,' said Barbara leaning forwards again to offer a plate of bread squares from a coffee table. I took a piece absent-mindedly and tried to remember when I had tasted the Fleury before. I asked Tom where he had bought the bottle and was surprised to hear that it was from somewhere so local.

'I thought you must have brought it back from your last trip to the Champagne-Ardenne,' I said.

'Boy! You know your wines.' said Tom showing me the label.

'It's just a hobby.'

I took the bottle and carefully read the writing on the back.

'What's the next sample?' I asked, handing it back.

'Do a blind tasting,' said Barbara. She took off the black chiffon scarf she was wearing and wound it around my eyes. Everyone cheered her on.

'Good old Barbara!' shouted Dennis Smart.

Tom poured a small amount of the next bottle into a glass and Barbara held it to my lips. I gently moved the glass down so that I could get my nose into it and took a deep sniff.

'Bordeaux probably a Pauillac,' I said carefully, 'but I couldn't say which year.'

'Bloody marvellous!' exclaimed Tom. 'You are spot on!'

Barbara unwound her scarf and kissed me on the cheek.

'Clever boy,' she murmured.

'You certainly pushed the boat out today Tom,' said I as I left. 'I didn't think we were going to get into fine wines just yet.

'What the hell, you only live once. Take a risk now and then, I say.'

Barbara followed me out of the door.

'Can I give you a lift?' she asked, 'I see you haven't brought the Jag today.' I hesitated, my shepherd's pie was calling and I was feeling a bit peckish. Still I did not like to appear rude so...

Once in the Volvo, Barbara pounced.

'I just want to show you something, come back to my house for a moment.'

'You don't live in a flat then?' I said as she let the clutch in with a fierce jerk.

'No I have this big place all to myself,' she purred.

The house was much larger than I had expected and Barbara parked the big Volvo on the formidable stretch of gravel outside the front door.

'The decorators have only just left. It's looking exactly how I wanted it, and I know you will love it,' she said as she opened the door and led me into the hall. I was impressed by her enthusiasm and thought of my own rather dank cellar at home with less than 50 bottles in their racks. Maybe I ought to have it painted up a bit too.

'Do you specialise in red or white?' I asked as I followed her up the stairs. I wondered why anyone would store wine upstairs, but kept quiet. Barbara seemed puzzled by the question.

'Well, pink mostly,' she said, 'This way.'

She opened a door and ushered me into a strikingly furnished bedroom in pink and grey with a large crystal chandelier above a long low dressing table.

'Well, what do you think?' she asked, 'Do you like it?'

'It's very nice.' said I , 'but I thought you meant rosé.'

'You are a strange man ! What am I to do with you?'

When I arrived home Sue was waiting in the kitchen.

'Who was that woman who brought you back in the huge car?' she asked.

'Mrs Garrard,' I said, 'from our group, she knows nothing about wine, nothing at all, and she called *me* strange.'

Chapter Twelve

If you don't learn to laugh at trouble, you won't have anything to laugh at when you are old.

The email from the estate agent in Naples came as a surprise to both of us. Although I had contacted him last time we were in Ravello, he had seemed so offhand that I did not expect him to have retained my little printed card, let alone given us another thought. The gist of it was that he had three villas in Ravello and Scala for sale and they all fitted the requirements I had mentioned, and he claimed that all fell into our price range.

'You must go,' said Sue, 'It will be easier for you on your own; and then I can come out if you find a suitable place, to, you know, confirm your choice.'

'But I have never gone on my own, especially on a mission like this.'

'Then it's time you learnt at your age,' said Sue firmly. 'Go, go , go...'

So I found myself checking into the Costantinopolis 104 hotel in the centre of Naples two weeks later with the minimum of luggage in my hand and my heart in my mouth. I reckoned that signor Palumbo, the *agente immobiliare*, could drive me about in his car rather than I take an hour's taxi ride to Ravello each day. Sue and I had stayed at the Costantinopolis once before, and found it very comfortable and a reasonable price.

The next morning Palumbo, who looked pretty ridiculous in a pale linen suit which stretched dangerously across a substantial stomach, collected me after breakfast in his silver Mercedes, and we drove along the motorway, past Vesuvius and up through the rather disreputable little town of Angri into the hills above Naples. The memories and feelings of all our holidays here over the last 30 years brought tears to my eyes. It is beautiful in many parts and yet quite ordinary and down-to-earth in others. I kept saying to myself, 'I must find something which will suit us.' as we climbed up the mountain. We levelled out before descending slightly through the chestnut trees on the new road to Ravello. The one that was re-surfaced for Hilary Clinton when she came to visit in the days when Bill attended the G4 summit in Italy.

The first house was in Scala, the tiny village on the opposite bank of the valley beside Ravello. Palumbo parked in the road below the steps to the villa and we ascended. I knew without any further consideration that there were too many steps. I imagined us carrying our groceries up. After counting every one of fifty-two stone back-breakers I told the *agente* that there was no point in looking inside the villa. Much surprised he followed me down the hillside and back into the car. We then drove up into Ravello itself but had to park below the piazza.

Now it was one o'clock and signor Palumbo asked if I would take some lunch with him, and where was my favourite watering hole. Naturally, I took him to Donatello's in the Via Roma, where I was treated like a long lost family member. We have known Donato the owner, for twenty five years or more. He made a fuss of us and gave us both a plate of mixed pasta to try, and followed up with his best crispolini with a litre of house white. To signor Palumbo's great surprise Donato refused to take any payment and we were ushered out after a cold glass of limoncello apiece.

The second villa that we saw was almost perfect. It had a wonderful view of the Mediterranean far below, framed in between the Stone Pines which are a feature of the area. Unfortunately it was up two flights of steps amounting to 60 or more, Palumbo had to stop and allow me up alone. There was no-where to park a car as all lanes leading to the steps were pedestrian only.

As we approached the third property I was not looking forward to being disappointed again. We were able to drive to it as it was on the lower road below the town and quite close to the new opera house, *el elefante blanco* as the locals called it. Signor Palumbo parked in the little private space beside the gate which had room enough for two modest cars. This time he took the key and unlocked the front door. As he let me go in front of him I entered a striking foyer laid in Carrera marble. It was a spacious two bedroom villa with two reception rooms either side of the broad hallway. A quite grand marble staircase wound to the right upstairs leading to a small mezzanine floor and the two bedrooms, each with en suite bathrooms. I knew at once that Sue would adore it as we had seen various similar apartments and villas on TV programs. I took several digital photos of the inside and then outside with my compact Sony. We came out of the front gate and I asked about the price.

It was being offered at €800,000!

'You said in your email that all three were in our price range.' My disappointment was pretty obvious by the loudness of my voice.

'But I thought that once you saw this villa you would be favourably smitten!' complained Palumbo. He wiped his sweating face with a tissue that he fished out of a top pocket.

How very Italian, I thought.

'I am impressed but I cannot conjure money out of a hat. We can't afford it and have money left to live on.

'It is called the Villa Inglesi.,' he said.

I got in the car without saying a word.

We got back an hour and a half later to my hotel in silence, until I stepped out of the car. Palumbo came around to shake my hand and to say goodbye.

'I am so sorry Mr Huntingdon. I have nothing more on my books.'

I phoned Sue with the news and went straight to bed.

The next morning I called signor Palumbo and after exchanging a few pleasantries, I asked if we could go back to Ravello and have another look at the third villa. He said that would be fine but it would have to be tomorrow. I was not averse to spending a day in Naples and so I agreed.

I walked around the city centre and then took a bus to the Via Nuovo Marina beside the sea and watched families on the beach and had a snack, a beer and an ice cream. It was strange to be on my own; like being on leave again back in the RAF.

I kept thinking about the Villa Inglese and wondering if we could really stretch to it. It was so perfect in every way.

Finally, exhausted by the walk and the sun I took a taxi back to the hotel and a light supper and bed.

By eleven o'clock we were back in Ravello having coffee in the square and soon lunch at Donatello's again. *Insalata caprese* followed by *lasagne,* the local red wine, which I never liked, but Donato offered free every time, and a *gelato misto.* This instance Palumbo paid the modest *conto* and we strolled down to the Villa. It looked beautiful in the midday sunlight. The tenants had already left to live in Sorrento, so there was no problem getting inside and having a much better look around.

'Would they take a much lower offer?' I asked.

'How much?' he asked with a very Italian shrug.

' €500,000' I said.

'*lei ride di me,*' he replied smiling.

'What does that mean?' I asked hopefully.

'In English I think you say, you are having a laugh.'

'Will you ask the owner?'

'*Certo*, I will try.'

We went back to Donatello's for a cup of coffee, then Palumbo took me back to my hotel in Naples.

That night, inspired by my visit, and my hopes for the villa, I sat in the hotel room and wrote a short story about my restaurateur friend. It was based on an incident that he had related to me concerning a pheasant that kept flying down into his garden.

Donato's Good Deed

In the Middle Ages, swearing in front of a live pheasant was an equivalent to the modern convention of swearing on a Bible . Either because the bird was considered so noble, or because it was thought to be an icon for the East i.e. the Holy Land.

The cock pheasant in all its fine colours settled on the wall just above shoulder height and walked slowly away from him. It looked ridiculous wiggling its bottom and tail feathers in an almost provocative way. It hardly seemed the dignified and noble creature from the Phasis river discovered by Jason and the Argonauts.

 Donato, despite his 78 years, could not help reaching out to catch the tail and the next thing he knew he had a struggling bird in his hands. It looked as if its dignity had been severely disturbed. He contemplated it dispassionately, thinking of the recent theory that birds were descended from dinosaurs. When you saw one up close it certainly gave an impression of great age. Donato liked to have high-flown and literary thoughts. He was very conscious of his Roman, and hence also Greek heritage.

Automatically, he wrung its neck, just as he used to do with his mother's chickens as a boy. The warm body rested on his bare arms with the silly head hanging down. A small trickle of blood ran from the beak. Donato congratulated himself silently. He still had the skill eh? It would feed at least four customers tonight, *Fagiano alla Crema di latte*. The commercially raised birds tasted like chicken, but the wild ones...*perfetto*. 'A dish for the God's' wrote Voltaire. He would recommend a fine Barolo to go with it. He walked down the shady street and gave it to his assistant chef Rafaello to pluck.

The bright Mediterranean sun never shone on Donatello's, the popular little restaurant in the Via Roma. The simple explanation was that the surrounding buildings were too high for the light ever to penetrate further than the topmost windows in the building. They were not occupied by the restaurant anyway, but were let out to temporary staff. The Amalfi coast is famous for its light and warmth, and Ravello, the small town resting on the mountain peninsula 300 metres above Amalfi itself, is still one of the best kept secrets on that part of the Italian shore. Its relative coolness in summer once made it the favourite haunt of the ancient Roman senators and their wives. Its exclusiveness made it an ideal hideaway for composers such as Richard Wagner, and that Hollywood star so famous for wanting to be alone, Greta Garbo.

Donatello's was opened just after World War 2 by Donato Giordano and within ten years was internationally known to an exclusive set for its quality and reasonable prices.

The pheasant would make around 60 Euros clear profit.

The restaurateur continued his interrupted stroll across the wide piazza and down the Amalfi road towards Scala the next village. He liked to take the air in the afternoon when most other people were having a siesta. It relaxed him after the lunchtime work. It also set him up for the evening meal preparation which was much more serious and demanding. His establishment was famous for its dinners, not just lunches. The cicadas sounded louder and louder as he descended the long hill. There was no other sound to compare with that Italian signal of summer heat. He passed the wrought iron gates of half a dozen gardens, and, reaching the halfway point of the sharpest bend, he turned as was his habit, and walked back up past the old vineyard and the rows of parked motor cycles, back into the piazza.

That evening, Donato was intrigued immediately he saw the two women in the doorway. The older looked about 45 but very well preserved and sophisticated, the younger one very similar in appearance, possibly the daughter. They were pale skinned in the best Italian tradition, and with dark soft curls framing their faces. The signora, wore a black business trouser suit, while the younger signorina looked attractive in a plain white summer dress. He led them to his own favourite table for four facing the door and took their orders. This meant asking them what they wanted as he never wrote out a menu; it had seemed too formal when he first started. Then as the business had flourished, the lack of a printed menu became his trade mark. He recommended the pheasant with the cream sauce, which they accepted, but opted for the cheaper local San Marco red wine rather than the Barolo.

Five minutes later, two men walked in who seemed the mirror images of the women. One aged about 45 and the other, evidently his son, matching the younger woman. Mischievously, Donato showed them to the same table and asked the ladies if they minded sharing as the other tables were booked. It was the kind of small social experiment that he enjoyed. They agreed, and the four customers soon introduced themselves and began to talk animatedly. Donato recommended the other half of the pheasant, and all seemed to go very well.

'My name is Cesare Rossi and this is Cristoforo,' said the older man.

'We are Bianca and Carlotta,' said the older woman.

' Sisters I presume?' asked Cesare.

'No, more like mother and daughter,' laughed Bianca.

'May I enquire which is which?' asked the young Cristoforo gallantly.'

With laughter all round, the wine was poured and another bottle ordered by Signor Rossi.

Donato watched discreetly from the other side of the room. He made sure that as soon as the pheasant was finished he was on hand to take their orders for sweets. They all had dishes of the gelato misto that Rafaello was so famous for.

When the bill was being paid, the elder of the two women asked if there was a good place to stay nearby.

They were touring the Amalfi coast they said, and Ravello seemed an interesting spot. The two men also said they were thinking of finding somewhere close by. Donato expanded, and opening his arms with a huge smile, said that his brother's hotel the Villa Cristina, just across the piazza, would be perfect and he could obtain for them a special price. After a brief telephone call to Alberto, all was arranged and the foursome bade Donato goodnight.

Back in the kitchen Donato blessed the pheasant and the good fortune it had brought to him and to the four lovely people to whom he had served it. He sat and drank a litre of beer with Rafaello and they congratulated themselves on a good evening's work.

The following morning Alberto arrived at the empty restaurant for morning coffee with his older brother. They sat and chatted in their amicable way. Donato still limped and suffered a bad cough from the German bullets he had received in the war. He smoked heavily which made his chest even worse. After a long coughing fit, only helped by a generous double espresso, Donato asked about the four guests that he had sent across to the Villa Cristina.

'Yes, they all breakfasted together this morning by the pool,' said Alberto.

'Good, good, and did they seem to be getting along well?'

'Very well, as far as I could tell.' Alberto drained his cup and stood up, 'And now I must be getting back. Rosaria will be wondering who I have coffee with every morning for the last twenty-five years.'

Donato slapped his baby brother on the back and gently pushed him out of the door as he had done every one of those mornings. 'I will come up and have a look at the love-birds later,' he laughed.

That afternoon, the two women and the two men were to be seen walking in the garden of the Villa Rufolo. This ancient villa is the show-piece of Ravello and like so many of the properties on this coast has passed from its original medieval owners to a rich Englishman who has restored it and designed the garden to be visited and treasured by countless tourists.

Bianca and Carlotta admired the immense variety of flowers on the high terrace and all four gasped at the view of the bright sea 300 metres below. There was a small orchestra playing in an alcove among the old stone ruins. 'Practising for the concerto tonight,' explained Signor Rossi, who seemed to know everything. The older woman turned to the younger man Cristoforo and gave him a hug.

'Thank you both for staying and sharing this wonderful place,' she said, her eyes sparkling in the sun.

Donato, who had spotted the foursome entering the Rufolo garden and followed at a discreet distance, was delighted to see his experiment working, although it looked as if the older woman was drawn to the younger man. He wondered if the older man had hit it off with the younger of the two women? What a laugh if that were so!

That evening the restaurant was packed with tourists. It was the height of the season and Donato was kept busy until they closed well after midnight. He half expected the four lovers to dine, but did not see them. He went to bed with the prettiest of his Rumanian waitresses that he had recruited through the internet, and forgot about other peoples' love lives. Jenica was only too delighted to be of service to her elderly employer. He was kind, clean, and divorced and enabled her to send 400 Euros a month home to her mother. Donato was a romantic and always fell in love with the latest waitress. Each one more attractive than the last, and none of them wanting to be a permanent millstone around his neck.

In the morning his brother arrived as usual for their coffee and chat at eleven o'clock.

'What about the two couples I sent you?' asked Donato pouring his brother's espresso.

'What about them?' asked Alberto resting both elbows on the small table and sipping from the cup.

'Well are they, you know, having it off?'

'Donato, you were always so coarse, I don't know where you got it from, not from mama that's for sure.'

'OK, but are they or not?' asked Donato. Having a young lover himself, he liked to share his good fortune with others.

'Yes, I suppose they are,' said Alberto, 'but let me tell you something. You may be my older brother, but you run a restaurant, you are not a hotelier.'

'What do you mean?'

'I mean that you do not study human nature as I have to. Those two couples, as you call them, are gay, omosessuale. The men share one room and the women another.'

'But I thought...'

'You thought wrong, and what is more, they left without paying their bill.'

Donato stood up disappointed, and wandered out of the door into the Via Roma. There was the swift sound of wings and the mate of the dead pheasant descended onto his shoulder and pecked at his undefended head.

'Get off you brute!' he shouted and pushed the angry bird away. 'You are no more noble than I am.'

Chapter Thirteen

Never miss a good chance to shut up.

On my arrival back home it seemed right to assess my general health and suitability for living abroad before making a final decision. After that trip I had assorted feelings. On the one hand I was disappointed with my failure to obtain a house; on the other hand I was really excited about the Villa Inglese. When I showed the photos to Sue she was as keen as I knew she would be. Even the tiny digital pictures on the Sony screen were inspiring.

But what about my fitness?

I can manage to stand firmly on my left leg to put on my right sock and smile with satisfaction at the achievement. Two weeks earlier, on four whiskies a day and a drug called a Statin every evening, I had been almost unable to dress myself. This abandonment of the pills which were turning me into a zombie, and the cutting of my whisky intake to one shot a day had made a genuine physical difference. I had been monitoring my own existence with all the dedication of a new convert to health and safety. I have acquired variolens specs which enable me to see both close-up and afar, and I now have two National Health digital hearing aids permanently in a drawer by our bedside, I am sure they will come in handy one day. I can now see, and dress myself like a nineteen year old instead of 85. I still enjoy driving my old Jaguar, and I am coping exceedingly well with the computer I have bought myself. During the whole time that I taught Art until twenty years ago, I had never touched a PC, but, as Scarlett has said encouragingly, it was not brain surgery and why not get with it?

The thing is, I have to take four prescribed medicines every morning for heart, cholesterol and arthritis and two or three garlic pills or fish-oil capsules which Sue has told me I need to stave off dementia etc .etc.

I read all kinds of stuff that comes through the post about insurance and equity release, which only serve to make me mad. The newspapers are no better. The ones with Gothic lettering for their names are the worst. England has always used antique calligraphy to give a kind of spurious respectability to bad news and health scares.

I loaded the Sony digital photos of the villa into my computer and we looked at them on the 21 inch screen. They did look marvellous. Eventually, after falling once or twice into a dreamlike trance during the slide show, I awoke and decided that we must have a huge clear-out sale and raise more money. There is a program on the telly called Cash in the Attic where ordinary people find the most ordinary items around the house to sell for huge amounts. Surely, with all our rubbish collected over 60 years, a search will bring up some old treasure or other?

It took two weeks of concerted effort to fill the back seat and the boot of the Jag with junk. I paid our ten pounds and we took a stand at the local car boot sale and got rid of the lot in three hours. It was fantastic, we made a total of £65!

Can't complain, it was £65 more that we had before, and it cleared out a cupboard or two. But it does not bring our house in Italy any nearer. We decided to do it again and this time choose some things that we could spare even although they might still have memories or some value to us.

Life gets very routine when you are over 80 and so the car boot experience was exhilarating. I do try to bring variety into my life. I sometimes have my coffee at 10.30 instead of 10 am. I buy a different sort of soap. Occasionally, I walk Jumble down a road we haven't used for a week or so, or have my hair cut a week late. Anything to stop getting into a rut. So this clear out has become most stimulating. I couldn't think what else we might have in the attic, except we don't have an attic, just a spare bedroom piled high.

'What about those twelve prints of old St Albans?' I asked Sue, 'the ones your mother gave us.'

'They are in the garage, but I am sure they're not worth much.'

'Never mind, we all have to make sacrifices,' I said. 'There's the ancient mat that Korky sleeps on. My father gave it to us.'

Sue laughed, 'Yes I am sure you can part with that without much bother, tourist tat.'

'It must be worth something. It came from Iran.'

'Yes, but it wasn't covered in cat hair in 1950'

I had to admit that Korky's bed had been through the wars.

We found a silver tray and an old-fashioned teapot and a complete set of dinner plates marked Royal Doulton on the backs. Sue came over to me and said,

'We don't have to go to Sotheby's with this lot, but let's take it to that small auctioneers out of town for a valuation.

Down at the club I was quizzed by all and sundry about my trip to Naples. Dave Bucknell was all agog.

'You were off the hook matey. Did you meet any girlth?'

'My visit was entirely business I assure you,' I tried to maintain a serious face on things.

'Yeth, monkey buthinetth,' laughed Dave and the rest of the aged but infantile crowd fell about with laughter.

'But theriouthly, did you find thomewhere you liked?'

'As a matter of fact I did.' Then I told them about the Villa Inglese and how beautiful it was, but a bit out of our league. A few sherbets later I was perfectly at ease and feeling no pain. Unfortunately my friends convinced me that I should not drive and so Dave took me home in his BMW. Why they believed that he could drive happily and I shouldn't, I'll never know, but it suited me fine. I phoned Sue and told her where I was. She said I could stay there for the next year as far as she was concerned. She sounded a bit miffed I thought. Probably a cold coming on.

The next morning Dave drove me to the club and I picked up the Jag to race home. When I arrived Sue was making coffee (decaf) for Beo and his new partner Magda. They were talking about our collection of bits and pieces for the auctioneer. Magda looked pretty huge with our second so-called grandchild. I counted eight chocolate biscuits that she ate with her coffee. When she saw my eyebrows, which involuntarily raised, as she leaned across the table for the ninth, she just murmured, 'I am eating for two you know.' More like four, I thought privately but said nothing.

'I could get a really good price for the silver tray for you,' Magda then said. Sue trilled, 'Oh could you?' and it was settled even before any official valuation.

After coffee Beo revealed why they had really come. He wanted to harvest his 'experimental' plants. Well, I had a shrewd idea that these plants were marijuana and not experimental at all. Then when Beo asked if we had noticed if any helicopters had been hovering over the garden recently, my suspicions were confirmed.

'Please take the whole lot away with you and don't plant any more,' I said firmly. He immediately went outside and I saw him later with a plastic bag full of a green substance which he was stuffing sheepishly into the back of his car.

Fortunately, their visit helped to obscure my overnight absence and no more was said.

Sue said that she had invited the Braithwaites over for dinner on Saturday, and did I have any nice wine to give them? I was pleased as Tom and Shirley Braithwaite were probably our oldest friends. Tom and

I had taught together both in school and later in Teacher Training College in Surrey. They were mad thespians and always in some production or other. They both sang as well as acted. This made them entertaining, if sometimes tiring, company. But we liked them both.

I spent a little time in the cellar, which is what we call our cupboard under the stairs, and came up with a white Pinot Grigio to put in the fridge and a French blended tipple from Provence called Chante-Clair that has recently become our house red.

The Braithwaites had a lovely daughter aged about 25 who was an aspiring actress. I think she had been in rep in Sidmouth for a couple of years, and in an episode of East Enders as a lollipop lady or some such. So I began the evening by pouring the wine and asking about Zoe.

'She's in Rome at the moment,' Shirley said proudly. 'In some film or other. She plays a young lady who has fallen on bad times. It's a romance.'

'You mean she is a tart in a skin-flick,' said Tom who always liked to call a spade a bloody shovel. 'But it's a living!'

I must say that Tom's comment got me thinking about how English people like to describe their jobs.

'What do you do then?' is the most common way for people to introduce themselves in England. You are supposed to answer with a brief description of your job, but in the most abstract terms you can employ. A straightforward reply stating 'I am a butcher' will almost completely destroy your standing in any room of Anglo-Saxons. The required response would be something on the lines of 'I am in the retail food business.' That is quite acceptable.

If your conversationalist wishes to push it further and you finally agree that you work in the meat market and occasionally carve up the odd chop for a customer that is fine. But to call a spade a spade in the area of employment at first acquaintance is still something of a taboo.

I was once at a party and asked by a future in-law what my brother did for a living. I said he was a welder. This answer being so direct was not understood, and so I was asked to explain what sort of business that meant he was in, was it some kind of financial term or involved foreign travel perhaps? 'No' I replied, 'He welds metal together in a factory.' There was a puzzled pause and then a relieved expression came over the face of my companion who was a keen golfer. 'Ah' he said 'You mean he is an artisan?'

As a primary school teacher for a year once, I began by telling people what my work was. I mean, I was actually quite proud of it. I found that nine out of ten folk who asked me what I did, would then say something like 'How very interesting; oh I just see someone over there I must speak to.' Later, I began to answer the question about my job, by saying that I was 'In education.' This was excellent. I got into some fascinating conversations, and most parents would ask my advice about grammar school selection or some such tedious subject. Subsequently, I found it more convenient to say that I ran a sex shop in Guildford and the tiresome requests for advice pursued altogether another path.

I remember asking a young man at a village hall social what he did for a living, and I was both impressed and intrigued to discover that he was a 'commodity broker'. By careful questioning and eliciting some exact descriptions of how he actually spent his day, I then worked out that he was in fact, a wholesale grocer. I certainly gave him full marks for that one.

It is just possible to get away with saying 'I am a doctor' but the post-war trend for higher degrees of all kinds, will sometimes encourage the rude reply 'Doctor of what?' This will be from a person who needs to feel superior to someone with a qualification. Most medical doctors these days keep fairly quiet about their jobs at first, on the grounds that the National Health Service belongs to all, and should you admit to being on its staff, you will be expected to give a consultation there and then in your hostess's sitting room. A friend of mine in the Air Force, who was a doctor, when asked any medical question while off duty, soon put a stop to this practice by insisting that the incipient patient remove his or her trousers immediately. Vets have of course, rocketed in social standing through the advent of James Herriot on television, and have possibly the highest social cachet in the land at the moment. Some medical practitioners are actually cashing in on this, and will describe themselves as vets at parties rather than as GPs. Thus in one bound they regain their lost status and avoid the problem of instant consultations as well.

If you admit to being a lawyer you run the risk that your questioner may be from another branch of the law. A barrister can hardly bring herself to speak to a solicitor, but may well be completely cowed by meeting a high court judge. Policemen almost always have to say that they are building contractors or that they manage a garden centre.

Anyway, I was intrigued to hear about Zoe's work in Rome. I wondered if we might email her and find out more. Any contact in Italy was worth pursuing at this moment.

Tom and Shirley gave us a full description of the play they were in themselves. It is a one-act offering written by one of the younger members of their theatre group. The story is about an old Auschwitz prison guard who is wondering whether to commit suicide in the basement of the nursery school where he is caretaker. He talks to his cat, played by Shirley. Apparently, the cat is the soul of a Jewish child who wants to forgive the old man providing he gives himself up to be a tin of Whiskas. It seemed rather modern to Sue and me but Tom and Shirley seemed quite taken with it, and expected it to be accepted for the Edinburgh festival fringe later in the year.

After a pleasant meal of lamb kleftiko, bought in a brightly coloured box from Waitrose, our friends left in good spirits to drive home to Guildford. They promised to send us Zoe's email address in Rome.

Chapter Fourteen

Lettin' the cat outta the bag is a whole lot easier'n puttin' it back.

As autumn closes in Sue begins to think about Christmas.

I know it's a cliché that Christmas starts in the shops around August, but it is no cliché in our house. Sue is stacking up presents, making Christmas puddings and getting me to fetch down wrapping paper and Christmas tree lights from the top bedroom and it's only September the 15th. I have barely recovered from the wettest summer on record plus my abortive trip to Ravello house-hunting. And now I am supposed to be helping with mailing lists, wrapping parcels for Australia to relatives we have not seen for 50 years, and cutting any holly I can find with berries on and putting it into the freezer. One of my fondest memories of my boyhood was writing to Santa on *Christmas Eve,* then getting excited because the time to be merry was the next day. Nowadays it's like a prison sentence or community service that hangs over your head for four months.

We delivered our pile of junk to the auction house nearby about two weeks ago and Magda has sent us £30 which is what she said she got for the silver tray, less her expenses. She didn't say how much they were.

This morning the auction house phoned me and asked if I would like to come in to hear their valuation. I said

I would come right away. It would save me having to spend the morning repairing a ten foot string of fairy lights which was about to electrocute Jumble.

When I arrived, Mr Benford, the valuer, asked me into his office and pointed to a chair. I preferred to stand.

'Mr Huntingdon, I am sorry to have to tell you that the total value of the pieces you brought in for us comes to approximately £275 .'

'Well that's not too bad...' I began. Then he interrupted me.

'In any event, there is one item, the Persian rug...'

'I do apologise for that, I hope no-one has caught anything from it. If so, I take full responsibility, you see the cat has been sleeping on it for some years now.'

'Mr Huntingdon, I assure you no-one has actually caught anything from the rug but you see we have a problem.'

'What is it?' I began to be a bit anxious, as I could see visions of a judge, a court room and large damages.

'The problem is,' Mr Benford went on patiently, 'I have had to send it up to London as we could not deal with it in house.'

'Surely there is no need. I can have it cleaned here.'

'No nothing like that, we didn't want it touched until it had been properly valued. We have sent it to Sotheby's.' I began to realise what he had been trying to tell me and groped for the chair that he had proffered earlier and sat down. He went on, 'I have just had a phone call from the Sotheby's expert and there is no doubt that you have a genuine ancient Persian Tabriz rug which could fetch up to £500,000 at auction, possibly more.'

'Wow! Christmas *has* come early ! ' I said.

Sue actually stopped putting pastry onto a mince pie in order to listen to my news.

'We must not tell a soul,' she said breathlessly, and I agreed.

'When do we get the money?' she asked.

'After the next specialist auction and then only if the rug sells,' I said, having been briefed on the proper response by Mr Benson.

'Why don't you ring up signor Palumbo in Naples and see if the Villa Inglese has been sold yet? He might hold it open for us.' Sue sounded excited, as if she had taken me seriously for once.

'Better still, I will email,' I said, 'It seems more businesslike.'

We waited for a full twenty-four hours for a reply, and when it came it was enigmatic.

'The Villa Inglese is under offer by another most excellente client with good bank accounts in Roma. I cannot offer to you by this week. Perhaps if this person is falling down at one time, I am email you for example next month or so,

yours with best times

Adrian Palumbo'

I thought it sounded slightly hopeful, but that may have been the usual upbeat attitude of any estate agent. We both decided it would be a good idea to put our present house on the market and so I asked a couple of local agents to call and give us an updated valuation. We have lived here for thirty years and kept it decorated and fully repaired the whole time.

The first agent took a quick look around one morning, spent around twenty minutes, which seemed a bit short for a detached four bedroomed house in half an acre of garden. He asked if he could use our lavatory and then came out saying he thought we might get about £450,000 on a good day with the wind behind us. I said that we had a quote for £740,000 only three year previously, and he shrugged and said, 'That was three years ago sunshine.'

I showed him the door pretty swiftly, I can tell you. I am no snob, but being called 'sunshine' by an estate agent does not make my day!

The next day a competent middle-aged woman arrived and spent an hour and a half inspecting the house and had a cup of coffee with Sue. We sat around the kitchen table and discussed what she had seen.

'Have you come to a figure?' I asked tentatively.

'Not yet my dear, I will be writing to you with our quote later in the week.' I thought that 'my dear' was a great improvement on 'sunshine' and escorted her politely to her Volvo Estate. She had the good manners to comment favourably on my ancient Jaguar which I always leave on the gravel in front of the garage, (mainly because of the junk in it which leaves no room for the car.)

I have always been a keen car driver, ever since my first little MG open top which I drove in the RAF. I failed the driving test when I left the Air Force but it did not matter as I had a Northern Ireland licence which cost ten bob in 1947 and required no test. I failed the driving test in England, not through lack of skill, as I had already been driving for about five years, but because I could not answer a question from the tester. It was 'What should you NOT do when *approaching* a zebra crossing?' I wonder now whether anyone could have answered it. The correct reply apparently, was 'You must not park on it.' But I still think today, how could you not park on a crossing when you were approaching it?

Anyway, the AA gave me a UK licence on the strength of the Irish one and it has been renewed every time since.

Two days later the lady's valuation arrived. It was £550,000. This was disappointing, but better than the other guy.

I have decided to do more painting. My friends have been very encouraging, although not inspired enough actually to buy anything. Selling art works definitely does not go with painting them. Hence the need for those semi-criminals we call gallery owners. These are the people who exhibit your works of art which you have slaved and cried tears over. They ask £1000 for a painting, charge you £200 for the framing, sell the work to some stranger at a discount of 30% and then take 50% commission. So the artist ends up with £150 if he is lucky. As my American pals say, 'Do the math.'

It is a bit cold for outdoor sketches in December, so I take a whole raft of digital photos from the window of the Jag and drive home to stick them into my PC. I then spend several days admiring my photographic skills while I put off even thinking about painting. Then I might be inspired by one of the pictures and, using the big screen I have set up in the spare bedroom, try to make an impression of the scene in watercolour.

At one time I used to measure all the objects on a photo with a ruler and end up with what was essentially an enlargement of the photograph done by hand. Nowadays, I use the snaps as inspiration and try to make my paintings as little like the photos as possible. This puzzles most of my friends and family, but excites all those in the local Art Club who maintain some interest in modern art. As neither style of artistic creation seems to sell very well, I have become indifferent to both. But I do like to fill up my time by waving a brush about. I no longer have to teach anyone, or explain myself. So all is well.

It is all serving to keep my mind off Ravello where I have done many paintings while on holiday and sold quite a few to the locals, well I say sold, usually they like to give me a small bottle of limoncello for a modest watercolour.

I did sell a piece of work there one afternoon. I was sitting on an old stone pillar opposite the bank on the square. I had just finished the painting when a shadow fell across the paper. It was one of my early works, very accurate and detailed. I looked up and saw a beautifully dressed man of about thirty in what must have been a black woollen Armani suit, dark glasses and accompanied by a muscular henchman who looked like, well, a henchman. He spoke quietly.

'You are English yes?'

'Yes.'

'You are artist yes?'

'Yes.'

'I like this aquarella, is nice.'

'Thank-you – I mean grazie,' I stuttered.

'You want to sell me this one? How much?'

I thought quickly. A bottle of limoncello cost about five Euros, but this guy did not look like a cheapskate. In fact he looked as if he was loaded, probably with ill-gotten gains. I usually got thirty Euros for a small watercolour when I did get money. So I said,

'One hundred Euros signor.'

He made a hand gesture to the henchman who took out his wallet and peeled off 100 Eros in notes immediately. I gave up the painting and the Armani man said, *'Grazie, grazie mille.'* and wandered off with his companion looking as pleased as Punchinello. Why he wanted a painting of the Banco di Napoli I will never know. But I reckon I could have got two hundred if I had asked.

Another holiday I recall, was when I had drawn a careful picture of an old house in Ravello in black and white pen and ink. I was quite proud of it and when a fellow English guest at the hotel spotted my work he asked immediately if it was for sale. I said yes of course, and we agreed on a price of my usual 30 Euros. He pulled out a huge wad of notes and said as he handed over the money. 'I sell chicken inoculation. It pays OK mate.' I asked where he was intending to hang the drawing.

'Oh it's for my little girl, she likes to colour things in with her crayons.' I had the presence of mind to suggest that he made some photocopies of my artwork and let her have a go at those, keeping the original. He said he'd think about it.

I keep telling myself that I should paint more abstract stuff. There is no doubt that these days, if a buyer has no idea what a painting is about, he will gladly pay a goodly amount for it. But if it is obviously a nice piece of local landscape or the picture of a well-known building, easily recognisable, then few buyers are interested. It is inexplicable. I am the first to admit that a fun-filled lively abstract looks better on a wall than a badly drawn poor quality picture of a thatched cottage with two ducks outside. But a well-drawn and well painted bit of realism must be worth something? As an ex-teacher of art I can tell from merely looking at any abstract work, whether the artist has talent or not. Unfortunately, many non-representative works are as talentless and badly drawn and painted as the old farmhouse with a spotted cow in front.

Nevertheless, big splodges sell for large sums. I really must have a go.

Beo has arrived down in the dumps. Magda has disappeared. He is distressed because she is pregnant and the baby is due in a couple of weeks. I tell him not to worry, pregnancy does this to some women and in any case we don't even know the father.

'Yes Dad but do they also always take your laptop and your complete collection of CDs?'

'No, that sounds bad. What else did she take Beo?'

'Well that silver tray of yours for a start.

'No, she sold it for £30, she gave us the money.'

'Dad, she had it properly valued, and it was worth £300 solid silver. That's gone too.'

I had to sit down and think. My main consideration was one of relief at not having a second completely unrelated grandchild to buy Christmas presents for. This was brilliant, well worth losing the silver tray.

'I am so sorry Beo.' I said putting on a serious face, 'why not stay with us for a couple of days?'

Chapter Fifteen

If you find yourself in a hole, stop digging

'Dear Mr Huntingdon,

We have re-examined your Persian rug and are pleased to inform you that its value is more likely to be nearer £40,000 than the previous quote. Our valuer at that time was suffering from some personal problems and has since retired from the firm. We are sorry if this has been of any inconvenience to you and assure you of our very best attention at all times.

Yours Sincerely,

Marion Partridge-Fortesque-Jones'

The letter from Sothebys arrived by this morning's mail. I watched our usual tall postman bending to push it through the cat flap in the back door. We have trained him to do this, in case we are out and there is a largish package to deliver. Although most of the time the letters are delivered at the front door by spotty youths whom we never see again.

Korky looked at me with a crushed and starving look, even though I had just dropped a hundred tiny biscuits into her plate. There is no satisfying some people. Perhaps she was missing her luxury pad. After all 40K is still expensive for a feline mattress

I showed the letter to Susie who was cutting up a cooked chicken.

'Told you it was too good to be true didn't I?' she said, sawing at a small kneecap.

'Yes but forty thou is not bad for supporting Korky's bum for her whole lifetime.'

'It won't buy us your Villa Inglese though will it?'

I had to agree, and decided to take Jumble for his walk while I tried to dredge up another wheeze to make money.

Being pulled along by an excited dog on a long lead is quite stimulating. I got to daydreaming that I was in the Arctic on a sledge drawn by ten huskies. It was cold but bright sunshine. The dogs were barking happily and my fur jacket and trousers were warm and I was twenty-five years old. I closed my eyes and imagined a huge expanse of snow as far as man could see. It was when I hit the tree trunk that I had my eyes opened for me. One of them was definitely going to be black by sunset.

It was time to talk to Beo. Since his split with Magda he has stayed in bed in his old room. He came down to tea today in my dressing gown and slippers. He was as subdued as I have ever seen him and Susie rushed about getting him a cup of tea and a piece of his favourite fruit cake. He actually hesitated for about a second before scoffing the cake, so I knew he was still upset. He then asked me a strange question.

'Dad, what made you marry Mum?'

Fortunately, Sue was out of the room by then, watering some plants upstairs. I had to to think about this quite carefully.

'It wasn't because I was in love with your mother,' I said. 'Of course we were in love, but then I had been in love four or five times before that. It is easy to fall for someone in that way. Marrying them is something else.'

'Really?' said Beo.

'Marrying involves so much more; sense of humour, same attitudes to money, similar education; similar desire for children, and you have to get on with each other's parents for a start.'

'So what made you choose Mum?' he persisted.

'To be honest, it was because whatever happened, I noticed she always remained rational and calm. My own mother, your granny, was a very emotional woman. Her constant threat to us all was that if we didn't toe her line she would be 'upset'; and perhaps without realising it, I was looking for someone the opposite. Added to which...'

'What?'

'I really admired her mother, your other grandma. She was so kind and nice to her husband. She always said that he was something in the city. It turned out that he was a cab driver. I thought I would be safe with the daughter of a family that stuck together. '

'So how am I going to find someone like that?' asked Beo.

'I can't tell you, but if you keep looking and let your head rule your heart, at your age, you should manage alright.'

Poor Beowulf, he had been hurt so many times by falling head over heels. He had always rushed into things and seldom had anything in his life worked out well.

It was time to think about Christmas again and Sue keeps asking me what I would like. I had seen an advert in the Telegraph colour supplement in the dentist's waiting room.

'Could I have a pair of tweed earphones?' I asked meekly.

'Certainly not! It too decadent for words.' said Sue sharply.

'Well I was only joking. I would really rather be surprised.'

'You will get your usual if you can't think of anything better.'

'Oh goody – socks.' I felt a warm glow of contentment.

'Why haven't you died?' asked Sue suddenly.

'Good grief, what makes you say that?' I was a bit shocked.

'No, no, I put that badly. What I mean is, how is it that we have both survived so long.'

'Must be your sense of humour,' I said, and we both collapsed with laughter.

Beo has gone back home now looking rather serious. He still has the job at the re-cycling centre which also allows him and his mates legally to sell small items that they salvage. It has resulted in him watching all the TV programs on antiques and collectables, such as 'Cash in the Attic' and 'Flog It', which are projected onto the public every day of the week. He is receiving an education at last that has some meaning for him.

Mr Benford, the local auctioneer phoned to tell me that the Persian rug had been returned from Sothebys, and that he would be putting it into their sale next Saturday if that was acceptable, I agreed. I also consented not to put a reserve on the rug. We needed to get rid of it whatever the price.

Sue and I went along at the appointed hour and were pleased to see that an illustration of Korky's bed was in colour on the cover of the catalogue.

The other cast-outs that we had put into the sale did rather well and made over £400 altogether. Then came the mat. I could see that Mr Benford was as excited as we were when he announced it –

'Lot number 363 a Persian Tabriz rug; who will start me at £10,000?'

There was a pause while the attendant held up Korky's old rug. It appeared absolutely ridiculous out there in the saleroom with everyone looking so serious. But the bids came, one or two from the floor but soon the internet took over and it seemed that at least three people were after it.

'£15,000 - £20,000 – £25,000

'Do I hear £30,000?' said Benford hopefully, but there were no more bids.

'Sold on the internet for £25,000.' and he crashed his little gavel down on his desk and that was it. Not bad for an old rug, but disappointing after the original estimate of half a million or so, and then later £40,000.

'So much for cash in the attic,' said Sue as we walked back to the Jag.

I drove down to the yacht club to give the news to the lads who had all expressed interest in our attempts to raise our villa-in-the-sun money. Unfortunately, Dave Bucknell was not there but the commodore John Wellings, was telling some anecdote or other at the bar when I walked in. He signalled to Jackie to pour me my usual, without even faltering in his story. I sipped the amber fluid contentedly while he continued...

'So this widow was so grateful to her husband's golf club down in East Kent somewhere, that she wanted to pay for a named garden seat or something in his memory. He had spent so many happy weekends playing down there. Anyhow, she came to me, as her accountant, and asked if I could arrange it for her. I drove down to the golf club to sort it all out and they had never heard of the bloke. There was no record of him even being a member of the club. For twenty years the blighter had been disappearing at weekends to this club that he had never joined. How was I to tell his missus? Then I got a letter from a woman living in a cottage near Folkstone saying she had been the *'special friend'* of this same fellow, but he had died and what was her position regarding the cottage, as she was only a tenant and felt in all conscience that she ought not to continue to live there...?'

Laughter all round, and one or two members who had boats that their wives did not know about, looked a bit shifty.

'What did the widow do when she found out?' I asked.

'Oh, she still wanted the memorial seat installed in the golf club. That was the story she needed to believe.' John Wellings added, 'It's not all dull being an accountant you know.'

I thought my report about the auction would seem a bit tame after that so kept silent. Talking of widows, who should come into the club at that moment, but Barbara Garrard from the U3A wine tasting group. I turned rapidly towards my dream girl Jackie behind the bar, but Barbara had spotted me and came over in a bustle of taffeta and clacking of high heels. Her violet hair was even more violet than usual.

'Ah Peter! I'm so glad to see a friendly face, can I buy you a whisky?'

'Barbara! How nice to see you in the Yacht Club. Do you sail?' I thought it best to take some sort of initiative.

'I've been a member for years dear. But when Nigel died I gave it up for ages. I thought it time I came back. But to answer your question, I never set foot in the boat. Nigel sailed and I was more of a social person.'

Barbara's very social bosom elevated in front of my eyes like waves breaking on a Solent beach. I gasped for breath under the powerful force of her mammary onslaught. It was obvious to the whole bar, I fancied, that she was thinking of her billows surging onto my foreshore. I thought of that pink bedroom of hers, and my stupid belief that she was going to show me her wine cellar. How could I have been so naïve?

'Well, I wouldn't mind a small one,' I said.

'Oh fiddlesticks! Let's have a couple of large ones,' she said firmly. From then on I was helpless in her thrall. She is one of those women who sail on relentlessly once they have got going. So we had lunch together, she had prawns while I had my favourite sausage and mash. She even told me about Nigel's moderate performance in bed. Too much information. I thought. I was reminded of a joke that Dave had told me about this very subject. I tried to remember it as Barbara droned on. It was about an eighty year old man who had gone to his GP about his erectile dysfunction. The doctor had hypnotised him and advised him, 'Just say 1,2,3 before getting into bed and you will be fine.' The old boy had said, 'OK but how to I get it to go down afterwards?' The doctor then told him to just say 1,2,3,4 and he would be back to normal. That night on getting undressed the old man said 1,2,3 and his manhood stood proud. His wife then asked sweetly, 'What was the 1,2,3 for?'

I started to laugh at my memory of the story, just at the time when Barbara was in full swing about some shop assistant who had insulted her.

'It wasn't funny Peter dear, she really thought I was a size twenty.'

'Sorry I-er-'

By this time my fascination for Barbara's outstanding assets had faded. I looked around and saw that all my friends had gone. The afternoon was developing into a storm outside and I told my companion that I really must get home.

Driving through the torrents of rain, I found it hard to make out the road. In fact, over the past three or four months I had been finding it more and more difficult to see properly when driving, even in the best weather. Turning a corner in the New Forest. I skidded, slammed on the brakes and the next instant I was in a ditch with the car on its side. Pulling up beside me was Barbara's Volvo. It was evident that she had been following me. She got out and ran across to where I was hanging unscathed in my strap.

'Dear man, are you hurt?' she leaned in and breathed sympathy and garlic butter from the prawns.

'Please just help me to get out.' I said sharply, rather irritated to be caught out as so incompetent a driver. By the time I had scrambled free, another motorist had called the AA, having seen their badge on my front bumper.

When the AA truck arrived, I supervised its righting the Jag and towing it to my own garage. Barbara insisted on accompanying me in case I was suffering from *post traumatic stress*. This was a term she had learnt from the television. I tried to explain to her that men of my generation did not have such a problem. We just got up and carried on. In any case we used to call it shell shock and it was considered a good wheeze for a couple of weeks' leave. But she was insistent and proceeded to drive me home in her car. Naturally, Sue was more concerned as to who this bosomy and blue rinsed female was, than what had happened to my Jaguar. Nevertheless, she thanked Barbara effusively for bringing me home in one piece and gave her some flowers from the garden. That is what wives do when they really dislike another woman I understand.

I went to the bathroom and took off all my clothes to have a shower. I did not have post traumatic wotsit, not in the least. But I was feeling a bit sweaty after all the excitement. What do I find? Sue has been using my shower and there is some awful shampoo on the rack made of *fruit*. Why do manufacturers put *fruit* of all things into soap? If I wanted to have avocado or raspberry juice chucked over my hair I could sit in some nursery school at dinner time. Also, she had turned my shower head about five degrees from its normal position, so that when I turned on the water it went straight out of the shower door.

After a refreshing ten minutes, four minutes longer than my usual time, I went for a lie down on the bed.

The next thing I know, my Sue was bringing me some nourishing soup in bed on a tray with toast and butter soldiers. Of course I said nothing about the shampoo, it would have seemed churlish. She had already rung up the garage who said that the Jag was virtually unharmed and I could collect it in 24 hours time.

Chapter Sixteen

When you are dissatisfied and would like to go back to youth, think of Algebra.

I don't know how knowledge gets around families but it was not more than a week before both Scarlett and Beowulf had arrived unannounced one Saturday lunchtime. Scarlett with Jenny and Ahab, and Beo with a new girl friend called Belinda Patterson, whom he had met through an internet dating site. She was a nurse/midwife aged about forty, divorced but miraculously no children by any previous. She was not Beo's usual type of leather-clad harpy with clunky jewellery and thigh boots. Belinda could only be described as mumsy. Her greying hair was cut short and she wore a tweed jacket over a plain cotton dress, low heels and brown tights.

We all sat down to lunch, mostly out of the freezer, as Sue had not had any warning that we would suddenly expand from two to six and a half. At least it meant that we had ice-cream for pudding.

'Well this is very nice,' declared Belinda as she cut into a de-frosted pork chop. 'I hear that Peter has had some luck in the sales recently?'

'How on earth did you hear that?' I asked, pretending a mild curiosity to cover my extreme irritation.

'Well not *hear* exactly. Beo and I watched the sale of the rug on the internet. It is quite fun you know. I do it all the time, although I must admit I have never put in a bid.'

'How can anyone keep anything private these days?' I asked, 'It's like big brother watching everything we do.'

'Never mind that Pop, what are you going to do with the money?' yelled Beo.

'We have our plans,' said Sue quietly.

'Exactly so,' I said, 'It's really none of your business.'

'I am very sorry Mr Huntingdon, I had no idea that it was supposed to be private.' Belinda was almost in tears, which was not a pretty sight in a forty-year-old midwife.

Jenny looked uncomfortable and picked up the baby to cover her embarrassment. She started to breast-feed Ahab, which served only to increase the embarrassment of the rest of us.

'I suppose you watched the sale on the web too?' I said.

'No, Beo phoned us if you must know,' answered Scarlett.

'So you all arrived like vultures today by sheer chance I suppose?'

After that, the meal was spoiled and everybody left the table. I took the opportunity to spoon four large helpings of ice-cream onto my plate and tucked in.

'I suppose you will be putting the cash towards your idiotic plan to live in Ravenna or some such,' moaned Beowulf when we all finally gathered in the sitting room to watch the TV.

'It's Ravello, as you well know,' I answered, 'and yes we shall be putting it away and saving for a *sunny* day.'

Sue then arrived with freshly baked scones and the only sounds heard were the munching of buttered treats interspersed with cries from little Ahab who had clearly detected tension in the room.

I collected the Jag from my garage the next day. Apart from some grass stains on the driver's door handle, it looked OK. I was going to buy some fireworks as it was November, and I know that both Beowulf and Scarlett still liked to keep up the family tradition of frightening every furry pet in the district on bonfire night. But I decided to wait and have Guy Fawkes on November the 7th because I had found, from long experience, that fireworks were half price or less on November 6th.

That evening I had an email from a strange name, a woman I had never heard of called Zoe from Rome. She said she had spent ages finding out about some bloke called Signor Caparelli who apparently owned the Villa Inglese in Ravello. I could not place this Zoe at all and wondered what business it was of hers to make enquiries about my villa. I smelled a scam of some sort here. We are always being warned about email scams. People pretending that they know you and getting huge sums of money out of your bank account. Zoe wrote that this Signor Caparelli was a suspicious character and that it might be wise to have nothing to do with any property that he owned. It was rumoured, she said, that he had strong M*f*a connections. What on earth was a M*f*a connection? There was a bit more about giving love to her parents and then the penny dropped! Of course, it was our old friends the Braithwaites' daughter. They must have asked her to make some enquiries for us. In fact, we asked them to. Oh dear! I must be getting old.

I toddled downstairs to tell Sue; who said that M*f*a was probably Mafia, and that Zoe quite possibly did not want to write the whole word in an email in case the CIA responded to it, like they do with keywords on the telephone. All this seemed a bit scary and I wondered if I should even reply to the email.

'Don't worry dear, I will give the Braithwaites a ring and tell them we have heard from Zoe and it was very kind of them to take the trouble,' Sue assured me.

The next noteworthy thing in our lives was that a small parcel arrived from Beowulf containing two bottom-of-the-range Nokia mobile phones. There was a note from him apologising for his outburst at the family lunch, and asking Sue and me to accept these upgrades to our non-tech existences, so that he might keep in better touch with us. We were both affected and yet nonplussed at the same time. It was an unusually kind thought on his part, but a mystery to both of us as to how they worked. We put the mobiles in a drawer until we could spend time working them out.

Our next door neighbours' daughter Penny, aged twelve, came in to ask if she could take Jumble for a walk the following day. Her parents, Luke and Ellen Russell, were good friends of ours and we were very fond of their five children. We called them 'The Russell offspring'. Penny was the youngest. Sue asked her if she could help us with the phones. Penny was delighted, and so patient, that in half an hour she had given both of us the confidence to try making a call. From then on we determined to use the little Nokias to stay in touch whenever we went shopping and so on.

Sue had to go to the hospital that afternoon for a blood test and so I dropped her off in the Jag and we arranged that she would call me when she needed picking up after the test. I went home and started to sort through my old videos. I have hundreds from those halcyon days when you could video TV programs and watch them later on. Not like today's awful digital stuff when you need an engineering degree to record anything. Three hours later, I wondered whether Sue had rung me. I then realised that I had not switched my phone on and Sue herself arrived at the front door fuming. She had walked the two miles from the hospital ringing my number every five minutes. I merely said that I had not heard her call and something must be wrong with my mobile. She did not speak to me for three hours. What Beo would have called 'a result'!

A few days later I went into town to buy a refill for my favourite fibre tip pen. I said we should try to use the phones again and Sue reluctantly agreed. I said, 'Don't phone me while I am in W H Smiths, it will be too embarrassing. Wait until I am in the High Street, then you can come in on the bus and meet me for lunch at the Chinese as a treat.'

I finished my purchase and walked to the restaurant, but still no call from Sue. I checked that my phone was switched on, it was. After waiting a full hour, I called her and she asked me where I was.

'In the restaurant,' I said, 'waiting for you to call.'

'You didn't call me to say you had left Smiths!' she cried, rather crossly, I thought.

'That wasn't the arrangement. You were meant to call me.'

'But you didn't want to be embarrassed. How was I to know you weren't still in the stationers?.'

By now she was practically climbing down the phone at me, incandescent with fury. I thought how good these little phones were to pick up such subtleties of expression. Anyway, she refused to come to town and I had to enjoy a quiet Chinese meal on my own for once. Again, I thought, 'a result!'

But I don't think that the new phones were helping our marriage as much as Beo had hoped.

The whole thing reminded me of when I was about ten and my brother was eight. We had tied two empty soup tins to the opposite ends of a 100 yards of string, using a diagram from The Children's Encyclopaedia, and tried to speak and listen to one another at the same time. That ended in tears.

Chapter Seventeen

Always drink upstream from the herd.

We may think we are unique individuals, no two souls alike, our personalized DNA coursing through our veins inside the blood that formed us, but I think we are probably herd animals. It is so difficult not to conform. When I threw up before my night time excursions over Germany in the 1940s, I used to think I was the only one, and I was ashamed and hid in the toilets. Later on, I found out that almost everybody did the same and those that didn't were either insane or lying. Those who appeared to be completely unmoved were called "Flak-happy."

I have never been so scared, before or since, as I was in those days of being locked into a metal tube over the Rhineland or Berlin; with nasty soldiers below chucking loads of sharp metal at us. The fact that I was dropping high explosives down on cities containing innocent women and children *never even crossed my mind.* The Nazis had started it, they had committed many more atrocities, they had bombed London and Southampton and Coventry indiscriminately. They had asked for it and they deserved it.

There has been such a lot of speculation and criticism in the last forty years; all by people who were not alive at the time. Total war is horrible. It is forced on you by politicians on all sides. Unless you have been through it you have no idea what it is like. When veterans of my generation say that they don't want to talk about it. It is not because we are strong taciturn heroes. It is because we don't want to be reminded of how awful it was. We don't want mentally to be put back into those days.

I can't help wondering sometimes how men like Beowulf, who grew up in such different circumstances, would react if it all happened again. But then we fought those battles so that men like him should not have to.

So far, over 400 UK troops have been killed in Afghanistan over ten years. At El Alamein more than 2,300 men were killed in two weeks. It make today's casualty figures, sad as they are, seem like a skirmish to those who experienced all-out war. It means we were successful then and can be proud of the outcome.

Mind you, I was not so proud at the time. I once decided to report sick before a particular operation. I was so terrified of going back in the air again. Three of us were in the queue to see the Medical Officer when we each re-thought the consequences of being labelled a coward and an outcast. We talked it over, and when it was our turn to see the doctor we each asked for some milk of magnesia to settle the stomach.

It takes much more courage than we had in order to go against the herd.

All this soul searching has come about because Beo, having watched some TV programme about it, has applied to join the Territorial Army. This act is so unlike him that I still cannot believe he is genuine. I think his new girl friend Belinda has made him think like an average mortal instead of remaining an aged hippie. She is, by any standards, far more normal a person than he has been used to. I am sure it has caused him to mature. At 52, he is at last thinking more like a 25 year old than a 16 year old, which was his previous norm. But surely, even a mental 25 year old doesn't want to be a part-time soldier, unless he can avoid it. Of course, as soon as he turned up at the recruiting centre he was told he had to be under 32 years of age, under 25 if he wanted to be an officer. Naturally, if he was already a Wing Commander or a Brigadier in the regular forces he might have stood a chance but...

My theory is that he knew full well that he didn't qualify, but for some reason he thought it would impress Belinda if he volunteered to lay down his life for God, Harry, England and Saint George.

I am slightly disturbed about the email from Zoe. We don't want to be mixed up with anything that smacks of godfathers or Marlon Brando. It would be upsetting for Sue to buy the Villa Inglese and wake up with a horse's head in the bed one morning. So I have decided to forget that possibility and try for a different house in or near Ravello.

Bad news.

I have been rushed to hospital early this morning with a terrible pain in my guts. Not since I ate a suspect pasty at our RAF skipper's 25th birthday in 1944 have I experienced such discomfort. Sue phoned for an ambulance at 4.15 and it arrived, I am told within eight minutes. I was quite incapable of looking at the clock myself. The emergency people could not have been nicer. The nurse even called me Mr Huntingdon, although she did slip slightly when taking my temperature by saying, 'Would you open your mouth *"For me."* I was wheeled into the X-ray department by a cheerful black porter with a broad Hampshire accent. Then a shock-haired doctor, about fourteen years old, in jeans and a sweat-shirt proclaiming 'Love me Tender', gave me a full briefing on what was happening. He said they were looking at gallstones, diverticulitis and possibly a tube blocked with poo. I did not think that this was a proper medical term, but apparently these days it is. He called me Peter, but was so pleasant that I forgave him.

The severe pain had subsided by six o'clock but I did not feel able to eat the dry ham sandwich that the nurse brought for me. I noticed that she had a little plastic badge with 'Dawn -ward sister' printed on it. I determined to call her Dawn at every opportunity and to try and see if I could ask her to do something *'For me'*. Unfortunately, the possibility never arose, as she went off duty at 8 am and I never saw her again.

They are keeping me in for observation.

The pubescent doctor came to see me again and sat down to give me the full briefing. It seems that I have probably got some kind of growth in the stomach and also a heart murmur. Too much cholesterol, too much alcohol and so on. I am a bit shocked by all this as I have prided myself on keeping fit. Sailing a bit and walking Jumble etcetera.

Sue came in and was very businesslike, not at all upset which surprised me. I suspect she is hiding her emotions to save mine. She says we must forget living in Italy, it is too late, and in any case we can't afford it. She also thinks that I will be better looked after by the NHS than in Ravello, where the nearest decent hospital is in Sorrento.

Scarlet rushed down to visit the same day and Beo came with Belinda who was marvellous and said she would drop everything and come and look after Sue and me. I was not to worry about a thing.

It turns out that all I have is a few gallstones. The consultant, who is hardly old enough for his testicles to have descended, says that they could blast them out with ultrasound, but with my diet of cheese, butter and cake, they would just come back again. So it's keyhole surgery and out with the whole gall bladder. Apparently the gall thingy is about the same worth as the appendix. They were both designed when we were all eating nuts, berries and teeny weeny seeds of barley or oats, and loin of sabre-tooth tiger on high days and holidays only. It can easily be spared. I shall only be convinced when I try out all my favourite food and booze and don't keel over.

The other test will be if I still have the strength to open a sealed plastic food packet of any description. Things have got so bad now that I am thinking of writing to the Radio Times to suggest that rather than prison for convicted criminals over 70, they should be made to live in a house where the only food they can eat is wrapped in hard plastic or sealed bags and they are not allowed knives or scissors. They would all be begging for a bowl of real 'porridge' or release within a week, except for those who hadn't survived and had died of starvation.

Back at home I was told to wait for an appointment for surgery within three months. I decided it was time that Sue and I wrote our wills.

We got together after watching Inspector Montalbano on a Saturday evening. With our obsession with Italy, it is the perfect TV program for us. It is set in Sicily and spoken entirely in a kind of Italian but with subtitles. The thing is that after about 15 minutes watching and reading the titles we both begin to feel that we can speak Italian like natives! But as Beo would say (natives of Australia perhaps!)

Be that as it may, we started to think about our last will and testament. In the past we had really wanted to leave whatever we have to blood relatives and this would exclude little Ahab which would be unfair, as it is not his fault that he is all kinds of bastard, being a modern baby. 'Is that important?' Sue wondered, as she pointed out that most of our royal family have uncles and cousins and so on, all conceived throughout history without benefit of a piece of paper. Should the little mite be christened Ahab Fitzhuntingdon perhaps?

So we decided to divide everything we possess equally between our own children and their partners and their children. That is to say whatever little bastards they might have when we pop our clogs. I was all for leaving a bit extra to Scarlett's partner Jenny. After all, she was a gorgeous young woman. She'd had the baby, and deserved something for putting up with our daughter, but Sue vetoed the idea, being the sensible one.

So Ravello is now a verboten subject. We will be staying in the UK for the foreseeable. In which case I intend to spend some time visiting parts of Britain that we have never been to; like Snowdonia and Market Harborough. We might even travel abroad but not too far. I find modern airports too much like Nathan Road, Hong Kong on a busy day. The channel tunnel appeals, if only because it takes you to a decent railway system. Say what you like about the Frogs, but they know a bit about engineering even if the grub is a bit rich for my taste. Maybe we could afford a modest cruise down the Rhine or the Moselle next summer.

Beowulf came round a couple of days after I got home with his aesculapian partner Barbara, who was the lady with the lamp personified. She might have arrived hot foot from Scutari, she was so caring and efficient. (Remind me to take an all inclusive tour of Istanbul and the Crimean one day providing there is no flying involved.) Anyway, Barbara fussed over me and made me comfortable, almost to the point of putting Sue's nose out of joint. But she was so genuine and helpful that Sue could not be upset for long.

'What did you see in my son?' I asked Barbara yesterday morning.

'He was so sweet and seemed to need a cuddle.'

'Well, that's a new one on me,' I said, 'we just thought he needed to grow up.'

'Well, that too, but I suppose I needed someone to look after.'

'You're looking after me.' I said.

'Ah, but you are only temporary, you are going to get better.'

'Or die,' I said

'Exactly.'

'You certainly know how to bump up a fellow's confidence,' I said, but I couldn't help laughing as I said it.

'We aim to please.' laughed Barbara; and I thought what a lucky chap my son was to have found her.

Beo arrived at the house later in the day and brought with him a huge bamboo cage with a fierce-looking Mynah bird inside.

'Present for you Pop,' he said, 'something to cheer you up.'

Knowing that Beo is intrinsically incapable of buying anything, I asked,

'Where did you get it?'

'Won it in a pub quiz last night in Reading, my local. Straight up Dad. Fair and square. I was the only person there who knew who Vera Lynn was.'

'Does he have a name?'

'It's a she, Dad, a female bird, but they didn't tell me her name.'

'Well let's call her Vera then,' I said. 'Thanks Beo, very thoughtful of you.'

Privately I thought WTF... Neither Sue nor I have ever been very good with animals. Korky and Jumble are rare exceptions and we have, in time, got used to their little ways and, what is more important, they have got used to ours.

But a Mynah bird?

'Does it speak?' I ventured.

'Not yet Dad, I thought it would be a nice

hobby for you to teach it. You were a teacher after all.'

There was no answer to that. I put the cage on the sideboard in the sitting room and determined to give it to Oxfam or Cancer Research or someone ASAP.

The next day I took the Jag to get petrol and stopped outside the little Tesco's on the outskirts of Romsey. Having narrowly missed filling up with diesel due to not realising there was a new colour coding system at the pumps, I went inside to pay. The girl Tracey, at the cash desk, has always been somewhat short on brains and can hardly make herself understood through a mouth full of chewing gum at the best of times. I stuck my Barclaycard into the slot and heard her say

'Put in your pin and placenta.'

'I am sorry dear but I have not brought a *placenta* with me.' I had no idea that some sort of childbirth offering was need for petrol.

I thought a little gentle sarcasm would not come amiss as she clearly had no idea what she was saying.

'Put in your pin and PRESS ENTER' she repeated, rolling the gum two or three times around her cheeks and looking at me as if it was *I* who was mentally retarded. The only thing to do was to pick up the card machine on its extended wire, put it to my ear and say 'Hallo, hallo?' This caused the girl's eyebrows to rise and her black ringed eyes to widen like golf balls. (I am only glad she did not tell me to "Strip down facing me" which is what the girl in the checkout at Sainsbury's had said the previous week. Just in time I realised it was my debit card she was referring to.)

When I left I considered that I had probably won on points.

It was no use even thinking about Ravello now. Clearly my health was not gung-ho enough; and in any case we hadn't sold the house or come even close to finding somewhere to live in the Naples area.

Although I now had to wait three months for the surgery, my Susie determined to treat me as an invalid. I was allowed to stay late in bed in the morning and watch TV. Unfortunately this coincided with several unspeakable advertising campaigns on channel four for foot powder, skin rash treatments and a 3D digram of how a nasal spray works, with full sound effects. I know that some people may benefit from this sort of promotion, but for me, before breakfast, it is just too much. I could not get out of bed quickly enough to reach the switch, and although Jumble had been sleeping quietly on the duvet, he had also hidden the remote without my noticing. I just had to turn away and groan into the three pillows that Sue had given me.

The sounds must have been much louder than I thought, because she came hobbling in anxiously to find out the problem, still soaking wet from the shower and as naked as the Rockeby Venus. This was all too much for Jumble who leapt up barking to defend me from this unexpected elderly unclothed lady. When Sue discovered that I was perfectly alright, she lost patience and slammed out of the door shouting that in sickness or health, it was time for me to get up.

I thought it was time I had a look at the garden. It had been some time since I turned the odd sod or pulled a couple of weeds out of the earth. I actually chopped some logs and had a go at cutting the lawn, but found that I was too weak to push the mower. I was tempted to drive over to the local garden centre but decided against it as it was still too embarrassing remembering the last time we both went there to buy some bird food. Sue asked the man if he had fat balls, and we were thrown out of the place for being obscene.

I wish my love would let me handle some of these things on my own. Unfortunately, when she does consent to leave me to make a decision, or lock the door at night, or even mend anything, she gets so worried that I won't function above the nine-year old level, that she inevitably does it herself anyway. So what is the point of my ever taking the initiative?

I did get the upper hand last Sunday though. We were in church together for the first time in years. Half way through the sermon Sue handed me a note on which she had written "I just let out a silent fart, what do you think I should do?" I scribbled back "Put a new battery in your hearing aid." Very satisfactory I thought.

Chapter Eighteen

Diplomacy is the art of saying 'nice doggie; until you can find a rock

Scarlet arrived without notice yesterday afternoon. We weren't expecting her and Sue went ballistic because we were out of bread and had no meat of any sort on the house. I pointed out that Scarlett was a vegetarian nowadays but that made no difference. Sue said that it was the principle of the thing. Once she has brought principles into the conversation I always concede.

The main point, however, was that Scarlett was dressed in what I believe are known as sweatpants and trainers; what we used to call a siren suit and plimsolls.

'Why are you dressed like a Man United footballer?' I asked, politely I thought.

'Oh Dad! I am in training for the London Marathon,' she said.

'What all of it?'

'Of course Dad, don't be silly. I am going to raise money for AIDS.'

'You mean, to help spread it, or to help cure it?'
Scarlett does not appreciate my brand of humour but I thought it most amusing.

'What do *you* think?' she asked. Now if there is one thing that gets up my nostrils it is people who ask that question. If I thought I knew the answer, I wouldn't have asked. What a lot of time would be saved if no-one ever said 'What do *you* think?'

Why not just answer the first question instead of prolonging the agony and answering one enquiry with another fatuous question?

'I think you are running the marathon to help spread AIDS of course.'

'Why do you insist on being an arsehole, father dear?'

'It's a gift I suppose.'

I always enjoy our little familial exchanges and so does Scarlett as she usually has the last word, and here it came.

'Get knotted Dad!' And it was time for tea.

Secretly, I admired my daughter for thinking of others for a change, and I only hope she will succeed in keeping this enthusiasm for exercise. If only Beo would do something similar. I have high hopes for the influence of nurse Belinda, but I suspect that any running effort by Beo will be fast and spurious.

Meanwhile, I have suggested to Sue that maybe we could consider moving somewhere other than Italy for our last few years. Somewhere civilised and warm, and where the health service is good enough to keep us from too much worry and one can guzzle down a decent drop of wine.

New Zealand sprang to mind but it seems that unless you have a child already living there you cannot get a residence visa. If you want to invest 750,000 NZ dollars in the country, you might be able to stay for two years. On the other hand, it would be like moving into Thomas Hardy's world but without the literary benefits.

Australia seems a bit easier for the over 50s but you need to have a lot of money, half a million dollars, and private health insurance as well as being of impeccable character. Which would be difficult considering Sue's propensity for scurrilous behaviour in garden centres. The other problem would be that it is full of red back spiders and seriously fierce sharks in the sea. Plus young idiots wearing banana hammocks and thongs (whatever they may be) who say "G'day sport" all day long.

France was another place suggested by Sue. She fancies the cooking, and the fact that very few young French teens have mobile phones. Unfortunately, my reaction is one of the disadvantage of living with people who can actually put up with Citroen cars.

The last time we visited France I had an unfortunate experience outside a village church. I was looking through a small pile of pamphlets on a table by the door. A rather shabby *citoyen* hovered over the offering and kept saying "ommelessa peppell." At least that was what it sounded like. It was embarrassing because he kept on uttering this mantra. Eventually, I realised that the pamphlets were about helping people who had nowhere to live, and "ommelessa peppell" was his attempt at English. Of course, I had to spend five Euros just to get away.

Scarlett has now based herself back at our house and is taking this marathon thing quite seriously. I can't help thinking that it has more to do with keeping away from the responsibilities of parenthood than a conversion to charity work. She has left her partner Jenny to look after Ahab on her own. She told me Jenny prefers it that way, which I don't believe for one minute. I just think that my daughter does not feel cut out to be a father. If I had the energy or the bravery, I would go up to Battersea to help Jenny myself. Ahab is a really cute baby and the older I get the more interested I have become in babies and tiny children. It must be because of the youth they have in such abundance and which I don't possess at all!

Anyway, Scarlett gets up at six o'clock each morning, fully booted and spurred in her special trainers and Lycra wear. She has a digital stopwatch on her iphone, and carries small bottles of water with a sort of teat thing for sucking it down on the run. Probably psychiatrists would see that as a jealousy activity, because Ahab is still being breast fed. She says she is starting off by running five miles for a month or so, and will then increase to ten, then fifteen until she works up to the full marathon distance a couple of months before the big day next year. I can only hope that Sue can afford enough of her high energy food out of our housekeeping money. Why is it that so many 40 to 50 year olds these days have not yet learned to support themselves?

One of our neighbours, Alan Comfort, came round this morning. Unfortunately I always smile idiotically when I see him because when Beowulf was very young, about six, he wrote about some of our local worthies for a homework project, and misspelt his name as Anal Comfort. I know it is silly and childish but I still giggle when I see him. Anyway, he wanted to complain that Jumble was worrying his wife. I asked what exactly was worrying her, but apparently that was not what he meant. It seems that Jumble has taken to grabbing Mrs Comfort's trouser legs when she goes out and practically pulling them off. I agreed that this could be very worrying, but I still seemed to irritate "The Cushion" as we had come to call the man.

'What colour are her trousers?' I asked.

'What on earth has that got to do with it?' he said looking dire and a bit pink around the chops.

'Are they red?'

'As it happens, yes they are.' he said.

'Well there you are. Tell her to take them off and put on a blue or green pair. Jumble is a dog who always attacks red trousers. It's something in the genes.'

Naturally, Anal, I mean Alan, thought I meant 'Jeans' and suggested that I was taking the piss. There really is no point in having any sort of rational conversation with some people. In fact, I sat down last night and set out a sort of poem about the way young people speak today. It is a kind of babble that substitutes for rational speech.

Modern Conversation?

I don't want to know.

They don't want to know.

At the end of the day.

You should get out more.

Get a life!

You got a problem with that?

Give me a break.

I need my space.

Know what I mean?

You are so dead.

It's all gone pear shaped.

What's all that about?

That is great.

Good or wot?

Whatever!

I can't get my head round this.

Absolutely.

As if!

No problem.

Having got that load off my chest, I found myself
having a really good conversation with my Susie in bed

last night. We were both wondering why old people, that is people like us, take so little interest in sex. It's not as if we were never keen, we certainly were; but we agreed that as time went by, age 70, then 80, our interest became more theoretical. After all, we had done it countless times by then, in innumerable positions and endless places. It's not that it became boring but to be brutally honest, it became extremely tiring and hardly worth the trouble. Good, or even poor sex, is extremely energetic. When you are young you don't realise how draining it is because it's worth it; also you might have a baby which is great. Procreating yourself seems like good idea when you are young and fit. Later, with a touch of backache and arthritis, reproducing your own species seems a tad theatrical. After a while it becomes unlikely and then impossible.

Sue still has a keen interest in young men with muscles and I love looking at girls' bodies clothed or unclothed. Neither of us though, really wants to do anything about it. It just seems like too much trouble and effort. Sue has become an aesthete and I have become a clean old man; or what Sue calls a DOB, that is a 'Dear old boy.'

Chapter Nineteen

*Live in such a way that you would not be ashamed to sell
your parrot to the town gossip.*

We have had a local election this week. Sue and I
always take up our privilege of voting even though we
each cancel out the other. The results, according to the
short-skirted newsreader on TV, are a triumph for the
UK Independence Party UKIP. They are a party
which promises to re-instate transportation, cut
Britain off from ever visiting France, Spain or Italy
again, and to bring back the groat as our national
currency. Of course they don't stand a snowball's
chance in a general election, but when it comes to
these local votes, the retired colonial police inspectors
and the ex Burma Shell directors, together with the
Hampshire forelock-pulling classes, decide that they
want to restore hanging for stealing bread and take
away the female vote. They hope that all Pakistanis
and Romanians will be shipped back to their estranged
relatives, in countries they hardly know, apart from
Rudyard Kipling stories. Then Britain will be left with
no doctors or nurses, and the plumbing will revert to
the state of Afghanistan's in three months. UKIP's
intentions in Education don't bear thinking about.
They are determined to reintroduce the secondary
modern schools for at least 80% of our children;
(which is what reviving the Grammar schools really
means.) Their backers are probably at this moment
buying up all the slates and slate pencils that India can

produce, ready for the big day when they can make a killing in new economic school supplies.

Beo phoned me again today on his mobile, or 'cell phone' as he insists on calling it. It beats me why he doesn't just take out American citizenship and be done with it. I shall never understand how someone on such a low income can afford a mobile. Anyway, I graciously condescended to answer him on our steam land line, and discovered that he has been plagued with 'cold calls'. I may have mentioned that I too have suffered from this pestilence and brought one or two to heel by boring them with my own health problems. Apparently, various organizations have got hold of his number now, and about four times a day he gets phone calls ranging from asking him to buy solar heating or double glazing, to offering to get his mis-sold loan protection insurance refunded. As he does not possess a house with or without windows, and has never been able to afford any sort of loan, these calls are driving him up the wall. He wanted to know if I knew anyone who could help. Added to which, most of the callers are Indians or Glaswegians, neither of whom speak any sort of understandable English.

As it happens, I have some ideas. The first one of blowing a police whistle loudly into the phone, was dismissed as not likely to stop the next call from another company. I also said that putting on a pathetic voice and saying 'I'm an old age pensioner you know' may work for me, but hardly for a strapping 52 year old. So I suggested he use a company that charges a small fee on the internet to help the sufferers of these marketing ploys. When you have signed up, you then have to appear to take a cunning interest in the caller and ask for more details of their company and phone number. When you have enough information to condemn them, you then report the particulars to this anti-cold calling firm. They in turn, contact the culprits and remind them that they are breaking the law, then frighten the bejasus out of them by threatening to prosecute if they don't take your name off their database. It seems to work for me, so I gave Beo their URL It has so far been the only internet offering that has been worthwhile.

Today, Sue is off to visit Stonehenge with some women's group or other. I believe they are comparing the relative provision of tea and bun facilities between the National Trust and English Heritage. All I know is that they won't have spent much time studying the actual henge, yet will return to each home with armfuls of coloured brochures which will adorn various sideboards and bedside tables for several months and then be thrown out by their cleaning ladies.

This means that I am free to pop up to Battersea to have some quality time with my non-related grandson Ahab.

I polished up the Jag until I could almost see my face in the doors and set off. On arrival, I was completely worn out from the effort of trying to find a parking space anywhere in London. I also forgot about the congestion charge, so will be expecting a fine any day now. I managed to solve the parking eventually, by leaving the Jag on the wide pavement outside a local post office and hoping for the best, as Jenny had told me that the number of meter maids had been drastically reduced due to government cuts.

Ahab was gorgeous and responded heartily to my cooing and chin chucking. It really is a privilege to have a baby in the family with all the fun and no responsibility.

Jenny and I had a great chat and she had made a sponge cake in my honour. I had no idea that lesbians could make sponge cakes and so was very impressed and grateful for the thought.

Looking at Ahab in his little ecobasket, I realised that the widely held assumption that there was once a golden age of innocence, sometime after Adam and Eve and presumably before the Greeks, was rubbish. The Golden Age is obviously just the memory of our own childhoods; before we grew to realise that banks were in the business of taking our money, not increasing it, and that 'beef' really means 'horse' where ready meals are concerned. Growing up should really be called growing down, as it seems to be downhill all the way once the teeth arrive.

I asked Jenny what she thought of Scarlett doing the London Marathon. She was pretty pleased about it. I got the strong impression that she was quite glad that Scarlett was out of the house and allowing her to have Ahab to herself.

'It's good that she is doing this for charity.' Jenny was stirring something in a saucepan and looking into the far distance as she spoke.

'Well yes... ' I started to say.

'She needs some space. I think the arrival of Ahab was such a surprise to her.'

'Yes of course...'

'I want her to fulfil herself in her own way.'

'But she has always been suspicious of charities. She just keeps the complimentary pens, and puts the free pennies from the begging letters into her purse, and never sends them any money. '

'I know, she is rather sweet like that.'

I began to have a new view of Jenny, I thought she seemed as daft as a meringue. I left with lots of kisses and promises to meet again soon. When I found the car it had two summonses sellotaped to the windscreen.

I think I went home a wiser old man but it was nice to be smelling of Ahab sick. There is something life enhancing and reassuring about the vomit of babies.

As I came through the front door, full of my intended report to Sue, I thought I heard voices in the sitting room. I often hear voices without quite knowing what is being said so I paused and concentrated. I don't know how Joan of Arc got on in this respect, but I hope she had better internal hearing than I do.

Then it became clearer.

'Give it to me, yes, yes, yes.'

'Stop it, shut up you stupid thing.'

'Oooh that's right, just what I needed.'

'For goodness sake..'

'More, more, oh darling, oh darling.'

'Stop it!'

'Touch me there, there, there, ooh yes, yes yes.'

'No more! I've had enough of this.'

I recognised Sue's tone of voice as I got closer, then I saw the wretched Mynah bird, Vera. Clearly the claim that it had not learned to speak was erroneous. The question now was WHERE had it learned to speak? I shall put an advert in the free newspaper tomorrow, and make it anonymous.

Chapter Twenty

Buy land. They ain't making any more of the stuff.

We shall have to think seriously about getting a small retirement home somewhere on the South coast. I wouldn't like to be too far from the yacht club. It would be nice to have my own small sailing boat again to take out in fine weather and to fiddle about with at weekends. I used to enjoy that a lot about a hundred years ago! Ah the memories come back!

Susie didn't usually come with me on those yachting trips, and so from the very first moment of stepping aboard I am single-handed, It can get a bit lonely, but the first 12 hours are so busy and with such a feeling of freedom that I don't miss human company at all. It is both   exciting   and   peaceful.   to   settle   into   the surroundings of the boat. To stretch out and feel the wheel, the sheets, the throttle lever to hand. All in the positions made intimate from previous voyages.

I satisfy myself there is enough tea, coffee, long-life milk. Double check that the batteries are both fully charged. Inspect all shrouds and running rigging and look at the main and kedge anchor stowages and chains. It is reassuring to find how the first day or two will fly by on board. How the routine tasks in themselves provide a kind of companionship. I look constantly for signs of wear and tear in the hope of being able to spend time mending or patching and making good. The state of the boat is something akin to the state of one's own body. To keep fit you inspect yourself for spots, sprains, overgrown nails, too much fat. You then scour, massage and trim, to put yourself back into shape. The boat seems to need the same kind of approach. The presence of wife or crew would be almost as embarrassing as if they had joined you in your daily ablutions.

The weather is changeable together with a stiffish breeze. The ventometer indicates force four to five. I spot fair weather cumulus, and what looks like *alto-stratus lenticulata*, according to my memory of that RAF instructor so many years ago. It means changeable I think, so that's alright.

So the first day single-handed draws to an end. I check the mooring, have a final look round under the stars, listen to the last calls of the cormorants. Lying in my bunk, I luxuriate in being within my own piece of the world. Maybe there is something in the theory of a vessel in water being like the womb. It is certainly as cosy.

I settle down to one of my travel books. Reading of Joshua Slocum spreading his tin tacks on. the deck to discourage the Terra del Fuegans, or battling through gales off the African coast, puts my puny trip into perspective. How did they do it? What extra energy and power to persevere did they have? And where did it come from? At this point I zip up my two sleeping bags, one inside the other, finish my large mug of Horlicks and wiggle comfortably down to sleep.

1 awake in the middle of the night to hear the loud trickling of the turning tide and those inevitable grunts and creaks of a fibre-glass hull suspended in its natural environment.

1 always wake early, the condensation from the fore-hatch dripping onto my pillow. I put on earphones and lie listening to Men of Harlech and the Londonderry Air on radio four until the first shipping forecast.

The wind has increased gradually and now the whole boat is vibrating. John Humphrys talks of gusts on the motorways. I start to feel more alone than I was yesterday. A pity Sue didn't come. She wouldn't have enjoyed this, but at least I would have had someone to moan to. Perhaps I ought to go back? The central heating and the telly are already beckoning.

There are still a few more chores to be done on board. Some rewiring of a bunk light; another go at the gas water heater that has not worked in two years. The day progresses and the tide turning again will soon be perfect. I twist the ignition key and start the engine for the final run. If I can give it say, twenty minutes, the batteries will be re-charged from last night's use of the reading light.

Another single-handed trip comes to an end. The cold February sun throws its long shadow across the pontoon as I climb out. Next time, next time perhaps, I will actually take the boat out of the boatyard and sail it. But the visit was fruitful, I got a lot done, and home is only half an hour away.

I think a small holiday cottage would be less trouble and expense.

Now I get an email from Beo. My eldest tells me that he has a new job. He has become an Avon lady. This is intriguing as Susie worked for Avon several years ago, just after I retired. I remember our neighbour Alan Comfort making fun of her chosen employment.

'What goes ding-dong and crawls in the long grass? Answer, a wounded Avon lady.'

I was forced to retaliate and to ask him who sits on a doughnut shaped cushion with a hole in it? Anal Comfort. We didn't speak much after that.

So, we may buy a cottage. Beo will sell us hand cream and shampoo at cost. Jenny will bring up our grandson, even though we are unrelated to either of them. Sue and Barbara will continue to look after me, and Scarlett will run the London marathon. Jumble and Korky will have to be put down eventually. As no doubt, will Sue and I. Altogether, quite a loving and normal family staggering on together.

END

www.ingramcontent.com/pod-product-compliance
Lightning Source LLC
Chambersburg PA
CBHW060810120626
46557CB00001B/160